This book is a gift from

THE SOHO CENTER
www.child2000.org

and

www.UVAChildrensHospital.com

For great children's literacy tips,
please visit
www.child2000.org/literacy

ATHLETE vs. MATHLETE

ATHLETE vs. MATHLETE

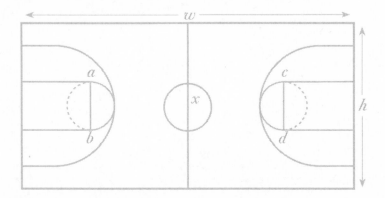

ATHLETE vs. MATHLETE

TIME-OUT

W. C. Mack

BLOOMSBURY

NEW YORK   LONDON   NEW DELHI   SYDNEY

First published in the United States of America in July 2014
by Bloomsbury Children's Books
www.bloomsbury.com

Bloomsbury is a registered trademark of Bloomsbury Publishing Plc

For information about permission to reproduce selections from this book, write to
Permissions, Bloomsbury Children's Books, 1385 Broadway, New York, New York 10018
Bloomsbury books may be purchased for business or promotional use. For information on bulk
purchases please contact Macmillan Corporate and Premium Sales Department at
specialmarkets@macmillan.com

Library of Congress Cataloging-in-Publication Data
Mack, W. C.
Athlete vs. mathlete : time-out / by W. C. Mack.
pages   cm
Summary: Owen wins the last spot at the local basketball camp, leaving his twin, Russ,
to join the Multisport Sampler camp, but while Russ is inspired to study various sports
and make sense of them, Owen is frustrated by not being the star.
ISBN 978-1-61963-302-5 (paperback) • ISBN 978-1-61963-301-8 (hardcover)
ISBN 978-1-61963-303-2 (e-book)
[1. Twins—Fiction. 2. Brothers—Fiction. 3. Sports camps—Fiction. 4. Competition
(Psychology)—Fiction. 5. Basketball—Fiction. 6. Sports—Fiction.] I. Title. II. Title: Athlete
versus mathlete, time-out. III. Title: Time-out.
PZ7.M18996Atm 2014   [Fic]—dc23   2013038577

Book design by Nicole Gastonguay
Typeset by Westchester Book Composition
Printed and bound in the U.S.A. by Thomson-Shore Inc., Dexter, Michigan
2 4 6 8 10 9 7 5 3 1 (paperback)
2 4 6 8 10 9 7 5 3 1 (hardcover)

All papers used by Bloomsbury Publishing, Inc., are natural, recyclable products
made from wood grown in well-managed forests. The manufacturing processes
conform to the environmental regulations of the country of origin.

For my absolute gem of an editor,
the Cheetos-loving Brett Wright,
who suggested we send the boys to camp

And for Mike Smith, who is no stranger to time-outs

ATHLETE vs. MATHLETE

Free Agent

My palms stung when I caught the ball. My sneakers squeaked against the hardwood as I pivoted left, looking to pass to someone.

Anyone.

Nicky was covered, Paul couldn't shake Nate, and my brother, Russ, was at *another* emergency meeting for Masters of the Mind. Man, I couldn't wait for the state competition to be over. After the weekend, Russ and Marcus Matthews could get back on the court and the Pioneers could get back to normal.

A full roster.

A winning streak.

"Let's keep it moving, Evans!" Coach Baxter shouted.

"I'm trying," I muttered, looking past the waving arms in front of me.

Nuts. There had to be somebody open.

Aha!

Mitch Matthews.

I fired off a bounce pass and started hustling down the court again. I could feel the sweat drip down the back of my neck as I kept an eye on the ball, which moved from one player to the next every few seconds. Soon, Mitch passed it back to me and I dribbled a couple of times before throwing it to Paul. He tossed it to Nicky Chu, who took the shot.

Swish.

"Nice job!" Coach shouted as he clapped his hands. "See how easy that was?"

We all nodded.

When Coach told us at the beginning of practice that he wanted us to pass the ball at least *five times* between center and the basket, I'd thought he was crazy. Like, seriously crazy. But when we actually did it, it totally made sense. All the passing back and forth meant we had to pay a lot more attention to where our teammates were and where we should be.

We had to look for open spaces and work together instead of sprinting for the net. We had to take our time and "be aware," as Coach said.

So far, so good.

"Hey, Coach, are we gonna have to pass five times in games, too?" Chris asked as he wiped his hands on his shorts. When he was done, they were striped with sweat.

"No," Paul said.

"It's just a *drill*," Mitch told him, rolling his eyes.

"Cool." Chris sounded relieved.

"A drill that will help you at game time," Coach said. "Now let's crank it up to seven passes. And don't be afraid to make some noise. Let your teammates know when you're wide open." He blew his whistle and tossed Chris the ball. "Communication is key."

"Communication," my best friend repeated quietly, "is key."

He passed the ball to Nate and I snagged it in midair. But the second I took my first step, Nate was right in my face, blocking me. I could have gotten around him and taken off, but I scoped out my passing options instead.

Just like Coach wanted me to.

"Right here!" Nicky shouted.

I threw him the ball and jogged toward the basket, hoping it would be my turn to score this time.

I got the whole idea behind good communication, but I knew for a fact that, as far as basketball goes, nothing speaks louder than points on the board.

After practice, I sat between Nicky and Chris on the locker room bench and started untying my shoelaces.

"Did you watch the game last night?" Chris asked.

"Seriously?" I shook my head, amazed he'd even ask a question like that. "When have I ever missed a Blazers game?"

"Good point."

"Williams was awesome," Nicky said.

"Yeah." I started smiling. "That final shot at the buzzer—"

"In *overtime*," Nate added, opening a locker door.

"Was amazing," Nicky finished.

And it was. It was the kind of moment I thought about all the time. Me, Owen Evans, saving the day with the ultimate three-pointer, a split second before the buzzer. My teammates leaping off the bench to lift me up in the air, the crowd going wild, the clip shown over and over again on ESPN, and—

"Owen?" Mitch Matthews's voice snapped me out of my daydream.

"Yeah?" I asked, dropping one shoe on the floor and starting to work on the other double knot. Why did I tie the stupid things so tight?

"Do you think you'll go?"

I looked up at him, totally confused. "Go where?"

Mitch looked at Paul, who smirked, then Nate, who rolled his eyes.

"Hoopsters," all three said at once.

"What? The camp?" I asked, surprised. "No. You've got to be like, fourteen."

"Dude, haven't you been listening?" Nicky asked.

"Obviously not," Paul said, laughing.

"Listening to what?"

"Mitch just said that they lowered it to twelve."

"Twelve years old?" I gasped.

"No, twelve IQ points." Paul laughed. "So you could *almost* make it."

"Very funny."

"Yes, twelve years old," Nicky explained. "*And* it's scheduled during spring break."

"Are you kidding?" I asked, my heart starting to pound.

Hoopsters had always seemed years away, just like college and the NBA draft. I'd figured I'd have to wait until high school to get my chance.

They were really taking twelve-year-olds?

I felt like I'd won the lottery, and I hadn't even bought a ticket! How cool was that? And the timing was perfect; school would be out for spring break and I'd be able to spend a whole week perfecting my game.

"I'm all over it!" I gasped. "Who else is signing up?"

Mitch sighed. "My whole family is going back to Minnesota for my grandmother's birthday."

"What about you?" I asked Nate.

"My cousin just had a baby, so we're driving to Montana to see it."

I couldn't believe what I was hearing! "You're gonna miss Hoopsters for a stinkin' baby?"

He shrugged. "I guess so."

"But he'll just sleep and cry the whole time."

"It's a girl."

"Whatever. She won't even know you're there."

Nate shrugged, so I turned to Paul. "Are you in?"

"My parents said it's not in the budget. They just bought a new car."

"Nicky?" I asked.

"We're going to Disneyland," he answered, smiling at the thought of it.

And that's what separated the men from the boys in basketball. I'd take Hoopsters over Disneyland any day of the week.

I was dedicated.

I was committed.

"Aren't you guys going to the coast?" Nicky asked, interrupting my thoughts.

Shoot! I'd totally forgotten about Cannon Beach.

"Yeah, you go every year, don't you?" Nate asked.

I nodded. "Sure, but once my parents know I can do this instead . . ."

They'll still want to go to the beach.

It was a family tradition, after all. Mom and Dad both took the time off work and we spent the week in a condo. It always rained and we ended up hanging out inside, playing board games and stuff.

It was fun and I usually loved going, but compared to

Hoopsters, Cannon Beach suddenly seemed like a big wet, windy waste of time.

"Well, I'm going for sure," I told the guys.

All I had to do was convince my family to go to the coast without me.

Easy, right?

The whole way home, I barely even listened to Chris and Paul talking about some crazy reality TV show I'd never heard of. No matter how interesting they thought it was, all I could think about was Hoopsters.

I imagined what the camp T-shirt would look like. How it would feel to step onto a legendary court and blow everybody away with my moves.

From there, it was easy to picture my NBA career and the shoes Nike would let me design, with my name on them. They'd be limited edition, for sure. Dark blue and white, like the Pioneers uniform, with something cool like "Evans 1.0" under the swoosh. Everybody would want a pair. No, two pairs: one to wear and one to keep in the box, in mint condition.

A collector's item.

"See ya tomorrow," Paul said, turning off at his street.

"Are you okay, O?" Chris asked when we were alone.

"Yeah." *Evans 1.0. How sweet was that?*

"Because you've been acting kind of weird."

I laughed. "I'm just excited about the camp."

"You're really going?" he asked doubtfully.

"Definitely." I turned to look at him and realized I'd never asked him. "What about you?"

"Hoopsters?" he asked, then cleared his throat. "I don't think I'm good enough."

"What are you talking about?"

"It's a pretty big deal, Owen. Serious, you know? I mean, Oswald went there and so did Wallace."

"Yeah, and they ended up drafted by the NBA," I reminded him. "Just like Hendricks, Bajard, and that rookie Masters who's playing for the Knicks."

"Exactly, they're pros."

"Yeah, but they weren't back then," I told him. "They were just like us."

"Just like you, maybe. You're a way better player than me, O."

It was true, so I didn't bother denying it. "So, you're just going to hang out at home?" I asked, feeling disappointed. I wanted to have a friend there with me.

Chris shrugged. "Kind of. There's a basketball day camp at the recreation center I might sign up for."

"Are you kidding me? Dude, this is *Hoopsters* we're talking about!"

He nodded and bounced the ball he carried everywhere, including the bathroom. "I know. Maybe next year."

I thought about how much fun me and my best friend could have in basketball heaven.

"Chris, that's crazy! Come on. Just sign up and we'll have the best time together."

Of course, we'd probably be split up by skill level on day one, but that was okay. We could still hang out during our free time.

"I'm just not ready, O."

When he turned onto his street, I sighed. It was another case of the men versus the boys in basketball. Turning down Hoopsters to hang out at the rec center seemed like the dumbest move Chris could make.

Sure, he might learn a few things, but there would be so much more to see and do at Hoopsters. And thinking he wasn't good enough wasn't going to make him any better.

But Hoopsters was going to make *me* better than ever.

And that's when it hit me. Maybe going by myself was a good thing. Maybe it would give me an edge over the rest of the Pioneers. Maybe being an awesome player meant staying one step ahead of everyone else.

Sure, I knew that working together was important and all that, but the truth was that every team on the planet had a number-one player. A guy who everyone agreed was top dog.

And why couldn't that guy be me?

The van and the car were both parked in the driveway when I got home, which was perfect.

"Hey, O, how was school?" Mom asked when I closed the back door behind me and dropped my backpack on a chair.

"Awesome," I told her, grinning.

"Hold on," Dad said as he walked into the kitchen. "Did you just say school was awesome?"

"Well, not school, exactly."

"Ahh," he said, then chuckled. "Practice."

"Practice was good, but the awesome part came after," I said, then told them about Hoopsters allowing twelve-year-olds.

"Wow!" Dad said, giving me a high five. "That *is* awesome."

"What's Hoopsters?" Mom asked, putting a super-stacked lasagna in the oven and setting the temperature.

"Just the best basketball camp on the planet," I told her when she closed the oven door.

"Sounds like fun," she said, opening the fridge.

"Totally." Catching her while she was distracted was probably a good move. I took a deep breath before telling her, "The best part is that it's happening when we're on break from school."

Mom swung the door closed and stared at me. "You don't mean spring break."

"Yeah," I said, giving her my biggest smile.

"Honey, that's our family time." She looked at Dad, then back at me. "I'm sorry, Owen."

Uh-oh.

"What? You mean I can't go?"

She shook her head. "The beach is a vacation for all of us. *Together.*"

"I know, but this is so much better than the beach."

"What's better than the beach?" Russell asked.

I hadn't even heard him come in.

"Hoopsters," I told him, then turned back to Mom. "This camp will be so much fun, and good exercise and—"

"We're not going to Cannon Beach?" Russ gasped.

"Of course we are," Mom told him, rubbing his already messy hair.

"Yeah, *you guys* are going," I said, nodding. "But *I'll* be at Hoopsters."

"Owen," Mom said with a warning tone.

"Dad?" I begged, knowing that he was the one with basketball in his blood. He was the one who played in college and got as excited watching the Blazers on TV as I did.

He was my only hope.

"I'm sorry, bud," he said, shaking his head. "Mom's right. Spring break is family time."

I couldn't believe what I was hearing!

"So you guys are going to kill my dreams so we can sit around and play Monopoly?"

"I like Monopoly," Russ said, fixing his glasses.

"And read?" I practically choked.

"What's wrong with reading?" Dad asked. "I've got a stack of mysteries set aside."

"Mysteries?" I asked. The only mystery was how I could possibly be related to these people!

"Murder mysteries," Dad explained. "I'm *dying* to get into them." He paused. "Get it?"

"Good one, Dad." Russ smiled, but all I saw were the seeds stuck in his braces. Why did Mom keep buying eight-grain bread? Why couldn't we have the squishy white stuff like everybody else?

And why couldn't I go to Hoopsters?

I hadn't convinced her yet, but I wasn't about to roll over. This was way too important to let go. All I had to do was make her understand how awesome Hoopsters was.

"I don't think you get what's happening here, Mom."

As soon as I saw her face get all pinched, I knew I'd started out wrong. "Oh, I *get* what's happening, Owen," she said.

"This is the opportunity of a lifetime," I explained.

Instead of saying anything, she gave Dad her famous you-handle-this look.

It was one of her worst.

"*Lifetime?*" Dad asked, but didn't wait for an answer. "I'm pretty sure it's held every year, O."

He patted me on the shoulder, like that would help.

"But I want to go *this* year." The words came out super whiny, but I didn't care.

"And I want all of us to enjoy our *family tradition* of spending the week at Cannon Beach," Mom said.

"Scrabble," Dad said, rubbing his hands together. "Card games. Hot-dog night. We all love that trip."

Not anymore.

"Never mind," I muttered. "No one cares what I think. No one's listening to me." I walked toward the stairs, wanting to get away from all of them.

"Of course we're listening," Mom called. "We're just not *agreeing.*"

"Forget it," I snapped, trying not to think about the pair of Evans 1.0s that would never exist.

Energy Transformation

I didn't give much thought to Owen's dashed dreams, mainly because my own were still alive and thriving.

After weeks of anticipation, my Masters of the Mind team was mere days away from the biggest challenge of our lives.

State.

Months earlier, we'd blown through the regional competition, barely breaking a sweat, and it was time for the next phase of our Masters' season.

And the pièce de résistance? Or, as my brother would say, the cherry on top?

We were absolutely ready.

We'd scheduled extra meetings and run through every kind of drill, challenge, and game we could think of, repeatedly. We'd practiced, prepared, and trained as though we were Olympians, and I felt to my very core that our efforts would be rewarded.

In the middle of science class on Wednesday, I caught myself imagining the closing ceremony at state, complete with medals and a podium. The national anthem played as my teammates and I placed hands over our hearts and sang those stirring and emotional words.

In English on Thursday, I could practically see an amazed crowd of friends, family, and complete strangers on their feet. I could hear the thunder of their applause as our team of five achieved the highest score ever recorded in the history of Masters of the Mind.

It made me giddy.

But during social studies on Friday afternoon, I stopped myself in the middle of picturing the team winning the national championship, then conquering the world with mental gymnastics.

I suddenly felt uneasy about the thoughts I was having, uncomfortable with the wildly confident voice in my head.

And, with a bit of a shock, I realized why.

I sounded like Owen.

I shook my head in an effort to clear it and spent the rest of class reminding myself what truly mattered. Masters of the Mind was about brainstorming, teamwork, communication, creativity, and a thousand other wonderful things.

The only goal for Saturday morning was to do our best and to have fun.

It was that simple.

× ÷ +

That night, I gathered my clothes for state, smiling at the team logo printed on my T-shirt. To my surprise, Mitch Matthews had designed it for us, and it was perfect. Silhouettes of each member of the team posed as *The Thinker* were printed in solid black on our emerald-green T-shirts. The frames of my glasses and my curly hair were obvious, just like Nitu's trademark braid.

I folded the T-shirt and placed it on top of the dark blue jeans that would match the rest of the team.

"Are you ready for tomorrow?" Mom asked from the doorway.

"Definitely," I said, turning to face her.

I was ready to do my best and have fun.

And if that led us to nationals? So be it.

Stop, Russ.

Mom smiled. "I hope you know how proud of you we are."

"I know," I said, smiling back at her before returning my attention to the task at hand.

"Russell?"

"Yes?"

"I mean *all* of us. We're all proud."

"Oh," I said, feeling my cheeks get warm. "Of course."

I'd never doubted Mom's support of my involvement with Masters of the Mind, but Dad and Owen had taken a little longer to come around. It thrilled me to know that they were truly behind me.

"Good luck," Mom said. "Not that you need it. You kids have worked awfully hard."

I nodded. "We're ready."

✖   ÷   ✚

After a sleep filled with dreams I couldn't remember, I awoke to a buzzing sound that wasn't coming from my alarm clock. A quick assessment indicated that the sound originated inside my body.

It was the buzz of excitement.

The big day had finally arrived!

I leaped out of bed, anxious to get started. I made my way to the bathroom, and while the steam from my hot shower clouded the mirror, it also cleared my head.

There were so many possibilities ahead of us! The team had already gone farther than any Lewis and Clark contingent that came before us, which felt like a great accomplishment. But I was dying to know how much farther we'd go.

Our dreams were limitless, really.

Once I was scrubbed, dried, dressed, and pressed, I headed for the kitchen, reminding myself along the way that the goal was to do our best and have fun.

"I made waffles," Mom said, slipping one onto a plate and passing it to me.

"My favorite. Thank you," I told her, although my stomach was filled with nerves and I wasn't particularly hungry.

Dad lifted his fork in a silent salute.

"So, how long is this thing going to last?" Owen asked, pouring a steady stream of maple syrup onto his butter-drenched waffle.

"Hold up, buddy," Dad said, taking the bottle away from him. "Save some for your brother."

"How long is what going to last?" Mom asked, joining us at the table.

"The competition," Owen said.

Everyone looked at me for an answer, but I could only shrug. "As long as it takes for us to be eliminated." I smiled. "Or win."

"So, like, *hours*?" Owen asked.

"I hope so." My heart was pounding with excitement.

"Great," he said, then groaned.

So much for support.

I took a bite of my waffle and discovered that eating wasn't going to be a problem, after all. In fact, I was ravenous. I finished it in what seemed like seconds and Dad got up to pour another round of batter onto the waffle iron.

"Big appetite this morning," Mom said a few minutes later as she watched me devour a second golden disk of deliciousness, smothered in syrup.

Dad let out a low whistle of appreciation when he handed me the syrup for waffle number three a few minutes after that. "Breakfast of champions. Huh, Russ?"

I certainly hoped so.

× ÷ +

The setting chosen for state was in downtown Portland, which meant limited parking. While my nerves jangled inside of me, Dad circled the same four blocks countless times while muttering about pay parking.

"I'm getting carsick," Owen moaned during one of the laps.

I had to admit, I was feeling a bit queasy myself.

"We'll find a spot," Dad said determinedly.

Mom checked her watch. "Russ is supposed to register in ten minutes."

"I can practically smell a free space, right up here," Dad insisted.

He was right, but a dark blue Mini Cooper zipped in just ahead of us.

Mom sighed as she checked her watch again. "Okay, Russ and I will get out here so he can register."

"What?" Owen yelped. "I'm the one who's ready to hurl."

But he was too late. Mom had already climbed out of the van and opened the sliding door for me.

As soon as I stepped onto the pavement, I gazed up at our venue. The Arlene Schnitzer Concert Hall, or "The Schnitz," was a complete mystery to me and I couldn't wait to look inside.

As we approached the front doors I wished the event was taking place at night. The vintage "Portland" marquee would be bright with neon lights, the streets packed with excited spectators.

Before I could get too wrapped up in the idea, I spotted two of my teammates.

"Sara!" I called. "Jason!"

They turned to face me with matching grins and I could tell they were as thrilled as I was that the day had finally arrived. Their T-shirts and jeans looked perfect, and I loved the fact that we'd decided to dress alike.

We'd look, sound, and act like a team, from start to finish.

When I reached them, I saw that Marcus and Nitu were already in the foyer, so we pushed open the doors and joined them.

Nitu greeted us by rhyming. "I can't believe we're finally here. This is the highlight of my year!"

Sara smiled and added, "I love that we *look* like a team. Don't pinch me if it's all a dream."

Mom gave my shoulder a squeeze and whispered, "I'll leave you to it, Russ."

I was still feeling both queasy from the circling van and anxious about the events to come, so I didn't have a rhyme on the tip of my tongue.

Would failing to rhyme jinx the team?

Of course not.

"So, it looks like registration is right over there," I said, pointing to a table surrounded by kids and parents.

Jason announced, "There's no time for running late, because we're here . . . to *dominate*."

"You're too much," Nitu said, laughing.

"But I'm right," Jason said, giving Marcus a high five.

After we checked in, we were directed to our assigned seats in the theater. As soon as we entered, I gasped. It was a beautiful setting, with enough seating for Lewis and Clark's entire student body, if not the whole school district.

The walls were covered with carved pillars; the seats were covered in velvet, facing a stage that would be the site of victory (hopefully ours).

For the next thirty minutes, a constant stream of spectators poured through the door and into their seats. I felt a little overwhelmed as the theater filled with noisy chatter. The audience was larger than I'd imagined (even in the best of my daydreams), but at least no one was occupying the balconies.

Yet.

I spotted my parents and Owen, right in the middle of the next level. Next to them were the Matthewses. While the adults chatted, Owen and Mitch Matthews barely spoke.

They were getting along perfectly on the court, but they hadn't quite become friends yet.

I was confident that they would, someday.

I scanned the lower seats, where all of the teams were gathering. Apparently, we weren't the only team who'd thought of matching T-shirts.

There were nine other schools in the competition, but most of them were from outside of Portland. The only familiar group would be the team from Beaumont, but I didn't see them anywhere.

When we tied with them at districts, their fearless leader, Peter, had announced that they would stomp us at regionals.

I'd already proven him wrong there, when we'd tied *again*.

But the time had come to remove Beaumont from the equation. Only one team could represent Oregon at nationals.

My stomach rumbled ominously as I tried to focus on the word association game the rest of the team was playing to warm up their brains.

Suddenly, the stage lights were turned on and the judges walked in single file to their chairs.

This is it!

The final step before nationals.

I took a deep breath and rubbed my sweating palms together as one by one, each judge was introduced to the crowd by the master of ceremonies.

Do your best and have fun.

"Are you okay, Russ?" Nitu whispered.

I nodded. "I'm fine."

"Because you look kind of—"

"Shiny," Sara finished for her.

"And pale," Marcus added, looking concerned.

"I'm totally fine," I assured them, hoping I was right. My stomach's sound track had moved from rumbling to gurgling.

The master of ceremonies spoke again. "I'd like each team to stand up for a moment when I announce them, then be seated." He glanced at a piece of paper. "Millbank Middle School."

A group of kids in orange baseball caps and yellow T-shirts stood and waved to their families in the audience.

"We should have done hats," Marcus whispered.

"The shirts are great," I told him. "Mitch did an awesome job."

Two more teams stood up when their names were called, and then I heard, "Lewis and Clark Middle School," over the speakers.

We jumped to our feet and I ignored the lurching sensation in my stomach as I waved along with the others.

"Beaumont Middle School," the master of ceremonies said.

I didn't see any movement in the lower section.

"Beaumont Middle School," he repeated.

I looked behind us, and still saw nothing. A soft buzz of conversation started to fill the area.

What if they failed to appear?

The master of ceremonies cleared his throat. "Last call for Beaumont Mid—"

He stopped in midsentence when the lights suddenly shut off. I heard Nitu and Sara both gasp in the sudden darkness. Then, there was a bright flash as a spotlight swept over our team and the rest of the crowd, as though it was looking for something.

What on earth was going on?

The light finally found its target, at the top of the aisle. A blast of music came through the speakers and a group of five familiar figures started walking toward the stage to the beat of a song I'd heard a hundred times in my own living room: "We Are the Champions."

I glanced at Nitu, who shrugged.

My eyes were drawn, against their will, back to the spotlight.

The Beaumont team wasn't wearing the T-shirts they'd had at districts, but dark suits, white shirts, red ties, and sunglasses. They carried their trademark briefcases, complete with the Masters' logo, and wore the smirks I was all too familiar with.

"You've got to be kidding me," Sara muttered as they passed our row.

"Oh, it's on now," Jason said, smiling. "We're going to take these guys down."

"Our only goals are to do our best and to have fun," I murmured.

Nobody heard me over the music.

$$\times \quad \div \quad +$$

I'd suspected we were in trouble as soon as Beaumont entered the Schnitz, and my suspicions were confirmed in the first round.

Word and math problems should have been our strong suit, but as soon as we sat down at our group table onstage, everything felt . . . *wrong*.

"It's bad feng shui, or something," Sara said, looking as awkward as I felt.

"Do you want to switch seats?" Marcus asked her.

Sara shook her head as one of the judges placed an egg timer on the table and the speed rounds began.

First, we had to make as many words as we could out of "acknowledgment," but we couldn't agree on whether it was spelled with two *e*'s or three. Then there were word problems, involving hours, mileage, and props.

The ticking of the egg timer was borderline sinister.

I felt sweat trickling down my neck while the glare of the lights practically blinded me. Every whisper and cough from the audience was amplified and I had a terrible time tuning out the noise.

When it was time for a break before the big challenge, it was obvious that we were all feeling disappointed in the first round.

"Let's not freak out," Nitu said. "We can still ace the challenge."

"Totally," Marcus agreed.

I nodded firmly, knowing we still had time to redeem ourselves.

Nationals depended on it.

✖ ÷ ✚

Onstage, all of the teams assembled the materials to build a bridge on their tables, and when the buzzer sounded, we all got to work.

Just as we'd practiced, I tied the drinking straws, Jason and Nitu tackled the popsicle sticks, and Marcus helped Sara with the string and paper cups. We had probably built thirty bridges since we'd first read the challenge, and through trial and error, we'd designed a structure that could support the single brick that would put it to the test.

At first, everything went smoothly, but as our fifteen minutes ticked away, the master of ceremonies announced how much time was remaining at regular intervals.

And when we had just three minutes left, I spilled our glue all over the straws.

"No!" I gasped.

"We've got it," Sara said, leading the team in cleaning up the mess and making sure the structure was intact.

"It's fine," Jason said as the final seconds dwindled away.

But we all knew it wasn't.

The judges tested each bridge, one team after another. Several crumpled while a couple managed to withstand the weight.

When our turn came, I was filled with shame and horror as I watched the bridge fall apart completely.

My stomach growled angrily.

While results were tallied, we stood under the hot, glaring lights next to Beaumont, in all of their smug glory.

The lead judge announced them as the winners and wished them luck at nationals.

My stomach performed a somersault, followed by a backflip.

I tried to swallow, but couldn't control the rising wave of sickly sweet syrup in the back of my throat.

Full-Court Press

The drive home from state was dead quiet. Mom and Dad had tried to cheer Russ up before we left the Schnitz, but he kept shutting them down by either grunting, sighing, or shaking his head.

We took the highway home and Russ waited until our exit before he finally said, "I choked."

"No," I said, chuckling. "You *puked*."

"Owen," Dad warned from the front seat.

"What? It was awesome!"

"I don't think—" Mom started to say, but I cut her off.

"It was the best revenge ever. I could tell that Peter kid from Beaumont was a total turd and when Russ nailed him, it was—"

"An accident," Russ snapped. "I didn't mean to do it."

"It was still awesome," I said, mostly to myself.

Dad waited for the light and turned left. "I'm proud of you, Russ."

"Can we please not talk about it?" my brother begged.

"What?" Mom asked, turning to look at him. "You did your best."

"And blew it," Russ said.

If "it" meant chunks, he was right about that. I had no idea chewed-up waffles would look so gross.

"There's always next year," Dad said.

"Please stop," Russ said.

"It's not that big a deal, Russ," I told him.

He turned to face me. "It's like losing the NBA championship."

Ha! "Yeah, right. Don't get too crazy, Russ."

"I'm serious!" he hissed at me. His nostrils were bulging out. "To me, this was *exactly* like losing an NBA championship."

"Honey," Mom said.

"Everyone at school is going to know about this." He blinked hard a couple of times.

Was he going to cry?

I guess if I lost an NBA championship, I'd probably cry, too.

I decided to cheer him up. "Okay, nobody at school even

knows Masters of the Mind exists, Russ. No one will know you blew it."

"Owen," Dad warned again.

"What?" I was trying to be positive!

"I let everyone down," Russ said. "I was supposed to be the team leader and I cracked under the pressure."

"It's not the end of the world," Dad said.

"It's the end of mine," he said, then went silent again.

I opened my mouth to speak, but Dad shot me a look in the rearview mirror, so I shut it.

Russ was in a funk for days after state and nothing seemed to pull him out of it. He hung out in his room alone most of the time, and moped around the house for the rest. All of his nerdy friends tried to talk to him at school and Nitu even stopped by the house twice, but he was still down in the dumps.

Of course, he kept studying like his life depended on it and he made it to Pioneer practices, but he just wasn't the same.

After a whole week had passed, it was my turn to set the table one night. Since Mom and I were alone, I told her how I felt: that Russ should be over the whole thing already.

"That competition was really important to him," she said.

"Well, lots of things have been important to *me* and I've had to get over them."

"Is that right?" She raised one eyebrow at me, like I was supposed to prove it.

"Yeah. I had to get over being outplayed by Dante Powers, getting benched when I knew I could make a difference in a bunch of games, and I even had to get over the Twinvaders when they joined the team." And I was just getting started! "I had to get over Hoopst—" I stopped myself, realizing I had a golden opportunity right in front of me.

"What's wrong?" Mom asked.

"Nothing. I was just thinking," I said, trying to buy some time while I came up with a plan. Something seriously genius was brewing and I only needed a second or two to pull it all together.

She opened the oven to check on the chicken. "Thinking about what?"

I waited until she'd closed the door again and turned to face me.

"Russ," I said slowly, knowing I'd only have one chance to get it right. "I'm worried about him." I paused to make sure I had her full attention. "He's spending so much time in his room lately and . . . I'm not sure it's good for him."

"Really?" she said, like she didn't believe me.

"Yeah. I think he needs a . . . change of scenery or something."

"I agree completely, Owen. That's why this Cannon Beach trip—"

"Won't help," I interrupted.

"What?"

I leaned on the counter. "Think about it, Mom. He's depressed already and the coast will be all gray and gloomy. I guarantee he'll bury his face in a book the whole time, and what good is that gonna do him?"

"He'll probably . . ." She paused for a second or two. "What are you suggesting?"

"I think it would be really good for him to go to Hoopsters. With me, I mean."

Mom groaned. "Are we honestly back to this?"

"Back to what?" Dad asked as he came in from the garage. "Hey, is that rosemary chicken?"

"Yes, and your son is claiming that Hoopsters camp would be good for Russ." She paused. *"And for himself."*

"I never said that," I told her.

She just gave me a long look, like she could read my mind.

She probably could.

Figuring it might be an easier sell to Dad, I took another run at it.

"I just think that he's got this big black cloud over him right now, you know?"

"Sure," Dad agreed, frowning.

"What he needs is a chance to blow off some steam, meet some new kids, and hang out somewhere besides his bedroom for a week."

"The beach is—" Dad started to say.

I made a desperate play by blurting, "Romantic."

Yuck.

The word left a bad taste in my mouth, like sour cream and onion chips.

My parents both stared at me like I was from another planet.

"What?" they asked at the same time.

In a flash, I knew just what to say.

"You guys never have any, uh, time alone. I know Nicky's parents went to San Diego for their anniversary and had an awesome trip."

"It's not our anniversary," Mom said, hands on her hips.

"I know, but just think about this for a second." I held up one finger. "You guys have a . . . um, romantic week together." I added another finger. "And Russ gets over this funk he's in and has a great time." I shrugged. "It's win-win."

"*Win,*" Mom said. "You forgot your own win. You get to do exactly what you wanted."

"Is that so bad?" I asked, with a big smile. For once, I wished I had dimples.

"Is it?" Dad asked, glancing at Mom, then putting an arm around her. "Is win-win-win so bad?"

I knew I was getting somewhere when I saw the look she gave him, like they were in a mushy movie.

"It *would* be nice to have some time together," she admitted. "And the camp *does* sound like a lot of fun for the boys."

Yes! It was working.

Russ walked into the kitchen, his nose deep in a book.

Without speaking to any of us, he took the milk out of the fridge and poured himself a glass. He was just about to head into the living room when Mom said, "Russell?"

"*Mmmhmm?*" he mumbled, almost to the doorway.

"Can we talk to you for a minute?" Dad asked.

He looked up and saw all of us staring at him. "What's going on?"

"Have a seat," Mom said.

Russ sat down at the table with a suspicious look on his face.

"We've been talking about a change of plans for spring break," Dad said. When Russ didn't say anything, he continued, "We think Hoopsters would be a lot of fun for you two."

Russ gave me a cold stare, then asked Dad, "Do you mean instead of the coast?"

"Well . . . yes."

"We think it would be a nice change of pace."

"Really," Russ said, looking from one parent to the other.

"And, as Owen pointed out, it's a good opportunity for Dad and me to have a little getaway together."

Russ turned toward me again, only this time he glared. "Wow."

"I know!" Dad said, totally missing that it wasn't that kind of a wow.

"I think they deserve a vacation, don't you, Russ?" I asked, to put the pressure on. I knew he loved Mom and

Dad, and it was obvious how excited they were about being alone.

He wouldn't mess that up for them.

He was too nice.

"Yes, they do," he said stiffly.

"So, you're in?" Dad asked.

"Sure," Russ said, forcing a smile onto his face. "I'd *love* to go to Hoopsters with Owen."

I knew sarcasm when I heard it, but I didn't care.

Before Russ had a chance to take the words back, I directed everyone into the home office to get the details from the Hoopsters' website.

We read all about the dorm rooms and cafeteria, the top-of-the-line coaches and equipment, and the fact that the office was open until six o'clock if Mom or Dad wanted to make the call.

Mom smiled at Dad and headed straight for the kitchen phone.

I couldn't believe how easy it had been to convince them! I wished I'd thought up the whole diabolical plan way earlier.

I got back to setting the table, only half listening to Mom's call. That is, until she said, "Only one spot left?"

I dropped the forks with a clatter and spun around to face her.

No way!

"Yes. Sure, I understand. I'll need to talk it over with the kids and call you back."

"What happened?" I practically screamed when she hung up the phone.

"There's only one space left for Hoopsters."

I felt my heart sink all the way down to the soles of my feet. The plan had been so perfect!

"That stinks." I groaned.

"And there are no openings for any other individual sports. But she did say there's a slot available for the Multisport Sampler."

"The whatty-what-whatter?" I asked, feeling a headache coming on.

"It's exactly what it sounds like, Owen. The same dorms, the same week, but a variety of sports instead of solid basketball or soccer or . . . you get the idea."

"So . . . ," I said, looking at Russ hopefully.

"I assume you'd like the basketball spot," he said, rolling his eyes.

"Definitely! Thanks, Russ."

He frowned. "I didn't say you could have it."

"Oh," I said, acting surprised. "I just figured that since *I* was the one who wanted to go to start with and I've been playing basketball *longer* and—"

"I get it," Russ said, crossing his skinny arms over his chest.

"Yes, I think we all get it, Owen," Mom said, leaning back against the counter.

"I've only played basketball," Russ said quietly. "It's the only sport I know."

"Exactly," I said, nodding. "This will be an awesome chance to see what else you're good at."

He raised one eyebrow at me. We both knew that the chances of him being good at anything else were, like, zero percent.

"Maybe Owen's right," Dad said. "Widening your horizons might be a good thing, Russ."

I could tell by the scrunched-up look on my brother's face that he was about to disagree, but when he saw Dad put his arm around Mom again, his shoulders slumped.

"Would you be okay with the multisport camp, Russell?" Mom asked, looking worried.

He sighed. "Sure."

"Wonderful!" Mom said, and rushed over to dial the number again.

"I see," I heard her say after she'd told the person at the other end that she wanted to register us. "Would you mind holding on for just a second while I check with the boys?"

I waited for Mom to ask what size camp T-shirt I wanted, but it turned out to be something else completely.

"What's wrong?" Russ asked.

"All that's left in the dorm is a single room or a double with one occupant."

"Huh?" I couldn't even follow what she was saying.

"One of us gets his own room and the other shares with a *stranger*," Russ explained, with an edge in his voice.

"Oh," I said, biting my lip.

"Who wants the single?" Dad asked. "You've got to make a quick decision."

Russ and I spoke up at the exact same time.

"Let's flip for it," he said.

"I want it," I said.

We stared at each other. There was no way I'd flip a stinking *coin* for something that important. I wasn't going to risk sharing a room with someone I'd never even met.

Russ crossed his arms again and I thought he was going to put up a fight or storm off or something, like I totally would have. But Russ never did stuff like that.

When he saw the way Mom was looking at us, he said, "I'll take the double."

Yes!

I couldn't stop grinning while I listened to Mom finish the call.

"Hoopsters!" I shouted when she hung up. I ran over to give her a hug and Dad a high five. "This is going to be the best week of my life!"

Mom walked over to give Russ a hug and whispered

something in his ear. He nodded and hugged her back, shooting me a dirty look over her shoulder.

Dad left to wash his hands for dinner and Mom was busy with the chicken, so I quietly said to Russ, "Thank you for doing this."

He gave me a long look and said, "I didn't do it for *you.*"

Of course, we both knew I didn't do it for *him* either.

Displacement

The night before Owen and I left for camp, I listened as my brother frantically raced from one end of the house to the other.

He was obsessed with his Hoopsters wardrobe, which meant digging his "best" socks out of the laundry hamper for a last-second wash. He tried on every pair of shorts he owned. He modeled countless outfits in the hallway mirror, as if he were seconds away from a *Sports Illustrated* cover shoot.

It was absurd.

He packed almost every T-shirt he owned, but Mom had to remind him to take more than *two pairs* of underwear.

A roommate wouldn't have survived a week with him.

I, on the other hand, paid far less attention to my wardrobe than I did to my reading list.

I'd visited the library and stocked up on a variety of science fiction novels, some of which were new to me, and others that were like old friends.

Once I'd resigned myself to attending camp, I'd decided that my primary goal was to simply *survive* it. And a small library would certainly help with that. Any moments away from field, court, or track would be spent losing myself in fictional characters and imaginary worlds.

And that was perfectly fine with me.

The real world had proven to be very disappointing (at least my role in it had) and I was having a difficult time forgetting it.

The fiasco at state had made me question everything I'd believed about myself.

Did I have what it took to be a team leader?

Was I smart enough to contribute when it counted?

And, most importantly, if I had another chance, would I still crack under the pressure?

The confidence I'd felt at school and at home for as long as I could remember had totally disappeared.

And my own brother didn't even notice! He was too busy folding JUST DO IT T-shirts to realize anything was wrong.

In fact, Owen was so selfish, I was amazed he was willing to share oxygen with the rest of the planet. (Of course, he hadn't been given a choice.)

I listened to him drag his overstuffed luggage down the stairs, grunting all the way. I smiled to myself for the first time in days and wondered if he regretted assigning me the "nerdy" suitcase with wheels.

I certainly hoped so.

✖ ➗ ➕

Mom made French toast and eggs in the morning and I'd never seen Owen shovel food into his mouth faster.

"Breathe, O," Dad said.

"I want to get going," he mumbled, spraying bits of egg onto my plate. "The faster I eat, the faster we leave."

Dad got up and rinsed his plate before putting it in the dishwasher. "I'll load up your bags."

He reached for the handle of Owen's suitcase and grimaced. "I'm pretty sure the camp has weights, Owen. You don't have to pack your own."

"Very funny," my brother said, scooping another forkful past his greedy lips.

"Seriously, what have you got in here?" Dad asked, struggling to lift it.

"Clothes," Owen said, with a shrug.

A dribble of syrup ran down his chin and I had to look away. Ever since that fateful day at the Schnitz, I hadn't been able to stomach the stuff.

✖ ➗ ➕

Camp took place at a facility called the Complex, which was about forty minutes from our house. When we arrived, it was immediately apparent that it was a very popular place.

Thirty or more cars were parked while parents unloaded kids and luggage in front of a gigantic silver building. It looked like something from the future.

"Whoa," I gasped, before I could stop myself.

The structure wasn't rectangular, but multiangled, with peaks and points extending in every direction. Even the windows had a silvery sheen and the sun seemed to bounce off of every surface at once.

It was extraordinary.

"Whoa is right," Owen said. "Look at that kid's backpack! I didn't even know Nike made one like that." He pointed somewhere else. "And check out the new Kobe jacket. Oh man, that is *awesome!*"

Dad started to look for a parking space, but Owen stopped him. "Dad, we can go in by ourselves. Everyone else is doing it."

Surprised, I saw that he was right. Kids were hugging their parents or simply waving before carrying their own bags up to a check-in area.

"Oh," Mom said, sounding disappointed. "Okay, well, we'll just say our good-byes right here."

I reached forward to hug her, but the seats made it awkward. Dad mussed up my hair and wished me luck. I didn't wait around for Owen's farewells, but got out of the van and lifted the back door to get my bags.

Once I had my suitcase propped up on its wheels, I waited for my brother, who could barely lift his bag out of the back.

As Mom and Dad pulled away, we waved to them and I took a deep breath, bracing myself for the week ahead.

"Come on," Owen said, leading the way to check in.

Every couple of seconds, he pointed out an article of clothing or piece of gear that I was supposed to admire, but I didn't pay any attention. I was too entranced by the beauty of the Complex.

And it only got better.

When we reached the front desk, we could see the emerald-green field below. It was perfectly manicured, like a golf course, and I wondered how many times a week it was mowed.

"What are you waiting for?" Owen asked, nudging me forward.

A woman with a long blond ponytail smiled at me and asked for my name. When I told her, she scanned a list and said, "Room two-ten, in the C Wing. It looks like you're sharing with Danny Sanchez."

"Thank you," I said, taking the information packet she offered me, along with a schedule for the week. When I saw the countless blocks of activities that filled each day, I tried to swallow the lump that had suddenly filled my throat.

Running at seven o'clock in the morning?

Soccer, volleyball, hurdles, and *pole vaulting*?

What on earth had I signed up for?

I glanced at my backpack and thought of all the fascinating books that filled it.

When would I have time to read?

I waited for Owen to get his room number and we headed over to the C Wing together, stopping every few minutes so he could put the suitcase down and rest his arm.

"Maybe we should swap luggage on the way home," he gasped.

"Maybe we shouldn't," I told him.

He stared at me. "Are you going to be like this the whole time?"

"Like what?" I asked.

"All pouty and stuff."

Did he understand what kinds of activities would be filling my week while he showed off on the basketball court?

Did he realize that I was facing seven days of zero privacy in shared accommodations?

"Well, if I am, it won't be your problem, Owen. It will be my *roommate's*."

He rolled his eyes. "You could have taken the single."

I didn't dignify that with a response. We both knew perfectly well that he wouldn't have let that happen.

"You guys are blocking the way," someone grunted from behind me.

I turned to see a giant, his arms loaded with gear.

"Sorry," I squeaked, moving to the side.

"Jerk," Owen whispered, once he'd passed us.

The guy spun around to give us a dirty look, but didn't say anything.

"Isn't this a youth camp?" I asked, watching him walk away.

Owen was too busy admiring everyone else's outfits to answer me.

Once we reached our building, we had to climb a couple of flights of stairs to reach our floor.

"I can't believe this place doesn't have elevators," Owen grunted as he lugged his suitcase up, just two steps at a time.

"It's a sports camp, Owen." I paused, then said, "Not a hospital."

"Whatever," he muttered.

I glanced back at him and saw that a lineup was forming behind him. A *long* and seemingly impatient lineup. The combined width of his body and his suitcase left no room to pass.

"Come *on*," somebody urged.

"I'd like to get to my room before Wednesday," someone else added and a few laughs followed.

Owen's face was flushed and I couldn't tell whether it was from the exertion or the embarrassment.

"Anybody into a pickup game before Orientation starts?" a voice asked the growing crowd.

I think everyone in the stairwell volunteered.

"I'm in," Owen called out, once he'd caught his breath.

"You might need a nap first," somebody said, and the stairwell was filled with snickers and snorts.

I waited for Owen at the top and we counted off room numbers until we spotted mine.

Taking a deep breath, I unlocked the door, hoping the room would be empty, at least for a few minutes. Just long enough for me to get my bearings.

Apparently, that was too much to ask for.

When I swung open the door, I saw a couple of bags piled on the floor along with no less than three basketballs, a laptop computer, plugged in (and playing loud music) on the desk, and a dark-haired boy lying on one of the beds, concentrating very hard on texting.

"*Hello*," Owen said too loudly.

The boy glanced up and grinned at us. "How's it going?"

"Good," Owen said, peering from one corner of the tiny room to the other. "I'm glad I got a single." He slapped me on the back and said, "Catch you later," before disappearing down the hallway.

"I'm Danny," the boy said.

I cleared my throat. "I'm Russ."

Thankfully, he leaned over to turn down the music. "Where are you from?"

"Here. I mean, Portland."

"Cool. I'm from Bend."

"I've never been there," I told him, moving toward the empty bed. I brought my rolling suitcase to a halt next to it.

"We can fix the beds tonight," Danny said.

I turned to him, surprised. "What do you mean?"

"Stack them," he said, smiling. "Like a bunk bed, you know? Then we'll have more room for people to hang out."

I nodded slowly but stopped when the words sunk in. "Hang out? What people?"

"Uh, other campers?" he said with a laugh.

I glanced at my backpack, feeling a sinking sensation that between the sports schedule and a "social" room, reading time was going to be hard to come by.

"I know T. J. and Big Mike will be here."

I was confused. "Do they go to your school?"

"Nah, they were here last year and they were at two of my other camps."

"Other camps?"

He nodded. "My dad sends me to at least five a year. Mostly in the summer."

"All basketball?" I asked, glancing at the balls.

He looked at me like I was crazy. "Yup. He's counting on me."

"Who? Your dad?"

"Uh-huh," he said, the smile a little tighter this time. "For a college scholarship." He sat up on the bed. "And then the pros."

I'd heard Owen talk about the glorious future of his basketball life, dreaming about ending up on the Trail Blazers roster, but this seemed . . . different.

"Aren't you in middle school?" I asked, amazed that a parent would have such high expectations. My dad loved the fact that Owen and I were playing for the Pioneers, but he wasn't expecting us to make a *living* from basketball.

"Seventh grade," he said.

"But you were here last year? I thought that opening the camp to kids our age was relatively new."

Danny nodded. "My dad pulled some strings."

At that moment, he stood and I tried not to stare.

Danny Sanchez was the height of a third or fourth grader.

And he was supposed to make it to the NBA?

Before I could say anything, there was a loud knock on the door. "Sanchez? You in there?"

Danny raced to open it and two boys took turns high-fiving him.

He welcomed them into the room and they looked me over, from head to toe.

"Russ, this is Tyrelle," Danny said.

"I go by T. J.," he said, smiling at me. His nose twitched, like he smelled something strange.

I turned to see the human skyscraper Owen had called a jerk in the courtyard giving me a cold stare.

"That's Big Mike," Danny said.

It wasn't the most creative nickname I'd ever heard, but it certainly fit the bill.

"I know you," he said, in a deep voice.

"Yes. I, uh . . . saw you on the way in, but we haven't actually met," I said, nervously sticking out a hand for him to shake. "I'm Russell."

He ignored the gesture and asked the room, "Who's ready to hit the court?"

"I'm all over it," Danny said, picking up a ball from the floor. "Russ?" he asked.

"I think I'm going to get settled in," I said. "I have to be in Gym Two for Orientation in an hour."

"Gym Two?" T. J. asked, his nose twitching again. "We're supposed to be in Gym One at ten thirty."

"For basketball?" I asked.

The three boys all exchanged looks before Danny said, "Yeah, for basketball."

"Oh, I'm in the Multisport Sampler camp," I explained.

"What?" T. J. asked.

"It's that other one, where you try different sports," Danny explained.

"Like baseball?" T. J. asked.

"It's different every year," Danny told him. "What are you guys playing, Russ?"

"Soccer."

"Cool," Big Mike said.

"Volleyball."

"Not so cool," Big Mike said.

"And, uh . . . pole vaulting and whatnot."

They all stared at me in silence until T. J. sniffed *again* and asked, "You signed up for *pole-vaulting* camp?"

I cleared my throat. When he put it that way, it sounded ridiculous.

Correction: it *was* ridiculous.

"No . . . it's actually part of the track-and-field component. It just happened to be offered this year."

"So why are you staying here?" T. J. asked. "This is the Hoopsters' dorm."

"The whole building?" I asked, surprised.

"C Wing," they all answered at the same time.

"A Wing is baseball," Danny explained. "B is for soccer, we're C, and D is football. I think your camp is in E."

"So, why'd they put you in here?" T. J. asked, with another nose twitch.

"I signed up late."

"Huh," Danny said. "Well, we should get out there before the courts fill up."

"Wait," I said as they moved toward the door. I saw a golden opportunity to distract Owen, who I was sure would appear at the door at any moment. "The guy next door would probably love to join your pickup game."

"Hold up," Big Mike said. "The kid who can't carry his own suitcase?"

T. J. chuckled.

Guiltily, I found myself reluctant to mention that he was

my brother. "I think it was very heavy," I explained, in Owen's defense.

Big Mike looked skeptical. "He can come down if he wants to, I guess."

"We'll be at the Freeman Court," T. J. said.

"If he can find it," Big Mike said, laughing.

Suddenly, despite all of his selfishness, I felt sorry for my brother. I wasn't expecting to enjoy camp, but he was counting on it. And the truth was that despite everything, I wanted him to have fun.

"He's right next door," I told the guys. "Room two-twelve. If you just knock, I'm sure he would—"

"Yeah, I'm sure he would," Big Mike said with a smirk. "But we need to get rolling."

Just before they left, Danny turned around to ask me, "You sure you don't want to come?"

I nodded. "I think I'm going to squeeze in some reading before Orientation."

"Oh . . . okay," he said, closing the door behind him.

I breathed a sigh of relief, until I heard Big Mike's voice in the hallway. "Squeeze in some *reading*?"

They all laughed, not bothering to knock on Owen's door before they headed for the stairs.

Sixth Man

My room was pretty awesome, even though it was kind of empty. Sure, it had a bed, desk, closet, and some drawers, but the walls were totally bare.

The place was going to be my home for a whole week, and I couldn't believe I hadn't thought to bring posters or pictures to make it look cool.

I looked down at my suitcase. The handle was about to break off and the thing looked ready to explode.

I might have forgotten decorations, but I definitely remembered everything else.

I unzipped the bag and a couple of my T-shirts fell on the floor. I shoved them into one of the drawers, then unpacked the rest of my clothes.

Rip City T-shirt. Check.

Nike hoodie. Check.

Blazers jersey. Double check.

I'd expected to have the sweetest gear at camp, but I'd already spotted kids wearing stuff I'd never even seen before.

I crammed the suitcase under the bed and put my hands on my hips while I looked around the room.

I was pretty much done.

I checked my watch and saw that it was only nine thirty. I had a whole hour until Orientation.

I looked out the window and saw a bunch of kids heading toward a big white building, most of them dribbling basketballs. They had to be playing pickup games.

Awesome!

I couldn't wait to show off my skills.

I checked the campus map and it took me a couple of minutes to figure out that the building everyone was racing to was Freeman Court.

I slipped off my old Nikes and put on my "good" pair, then switched to my favorite Blazers T-shirt. There was a mirror on the back of my door, so I stood in front of it.

I looked ready.

I hadn't brought a ball because I figured they'd have a thousand at camp, so I headed out.

When I walked by Russ's door on the way to the stairs, I knocked.

"Who is it?" he asked.

"Who do you think?"

It took him a minute to open the door. "What's going on?"

"Everybody's heading to Freeman Court to play before Orientation."

He looked surprised. "Oh, they invited you?"

"Who? *What?* No," I said, shaking my head. "You don't have to be *invited*, Russ."

"Oh." He frowned.

"So?"

"So what?" he asked, fixing his glasses.

"So, are you coming?" I asked, starting to get ticked off. It was like we weren't even speaking the same language.

"No, I'm going to read for a bit."

I stared at him. "You're kidding, right?"

He held up a book with a bunch of stars and junk on the cover. His finger was marking a page. "I'd like to finish this chapter."

"Russ, you're at Hoopsters!"

He shook his head. "No, *you're* at Hoopsters. *I'm* at the Multisport Sampler camp."

"You know what I mean."

The thing was, I kind of wanted to walk into Freeman Court with somebody, even if it was only Russ.

I tried another angle. "Mom and Dad spent a bunch of money to send us here." He didn't say anything, so I kept going. "If you're just gonna read, you could have done that at home."

He gave me a long stare. "I know that. I also could have done that *at Cannon Beach*."

"Come on, Russ. Don't be a baby."

"I'll see you later," he said, starting to close the door.

"I'm serious, Russ—"

"So am I," he said as it clicked shut.

Fine.

Whatever.

I'd go to Freeman Court by myself, and when I walked in the door, I'd have nothing but swagger. I was in paradise, and I wasn't going to let Russ's crummy attitude ruin it for me.

I hustled down the stairs and crossed the courtyard, making it to the court in under a minute. I took a deep breath and opened the double doors, ready to work some magic.

When I walked inside, I saw that it was actually two courts, and both were surrounded by kids watching games. I walked around the edge of the crowd, nodding hello to kids when they looked at me. Most of them nodded back or said, "hey," which was cool.

I found a spot at the edge of one court and watched as a guy about my age in a red vest dribbled a ball between his legs then threw a behind-the-back pass to another player. The other red vest caught it, took a couple of steps, and made a sweet three-pointer.

Whoa!

Instead of high-fiving like the Pioneers always did, the scoring team bumped fists. Just like the pros.

There was barely a pause in the action and the guard for the other team dribbled down the court, dodging in and out of the defending players like they were standing still.

"Over here," someone shouted and the ball soared through the air, right into his hands.

They hadn't even practiced together yet!

Coach Baxter would have been super impressed with the communication *and* the ball handling.

For the next few minutes I watched the game, amazed at how awesome some of the guys were. It was weird, though, because I'd been kind of expecting to . . . dominate.

A couple of Reds switched out and I recognized Russ's roommate when he got into position. I hadn't noticed how short he was when I met him. Of course, he'd been lying down, but still.

"Danny Sanchez," the kid next to me whispered. "He's awesome."

I found that hard to believe until he got control of the ball and turned into a human tornado. He spun, dodged, dribbled, and scored in seconds, and the crowd went nuts, like they weren't players themselves, but *fans*.

"Wow," I said, shocked.

A tall kid got the ball and started working his way toward the basket. He was smoother than smooth and when he glided across the floor, I couldn't believe he was just a kid.

"Tyrelle Johnson," the guy next to me said as he made an unbelievable jump shot.

I was impressed. Seriously impressed.

But I was also ready to get out there myself.

I walked toward the Reds' bench, since they seemed to be the better team, and asked the kid at the end, "You got room for one more?"

"There's a lineup," he said, pointing to a group of guys behind him.

"Cool," I said, even though it wasn't.

I tried the other bench, with no luck. I made my way over to the other court, where I decided to try a different strategy.

I couldn't see any extra vests lying around, so I walked up to the other team's bench. I stood next to the kid at the end. "Slide down a little, would ya?"

He glanced over at me and shuffled down to make room. As soon as I sat down, I felt like I was exactly where I needed to be. I didn't come to Hoopsters to be part of an audience. I came to *play*.

I looked back at the crowd of kids watching and realized it was another case of the men versus the boys in basketball.

You have to be aggressive.

I watched for a few minutes as guys traded off the bench, and when I saw my chance, I jumped up, ready for action.

"Hey," the kid next to me called out. "You can't do that!" But it was too late. I was already in the game.

I jogged down the court, happy to be in the mix. The ball was passed to me and I started dribbling like it was the most natural thing in the world.

Which it was.

I easily whipped around the Red who was in my face and kept going.

"I'm open!" one of my new teammates shouted.

I thought about Coach Baxter's five and seven passes, but I had everything under control. I kept dribbling, keeping one eye on the basket and the other on the opposing team.

It felt pretty awesome, knowing that everyone was watching me and I had the chance to prove myself before camp even started.

I dodged another Red, no problem, and dribbled a few steps closer to the basket.

Should I go in for a layup, or wow the crowd with a three-pointer?

The answer was obvious. It was *Hoopsters*.

I got into position for a three-point shot I'd made a thousand times before (or maybe twenty). But just as I was about to release the ball, an arm reached over my head and knocked it loose. It bounced once, and I moved to grab it, but the guy pushed past me and took possession.

"What was that?" one of my teammates asked as the ball thief took off down the court.

I didn't have an answer for him, so I ran after the ball, hoping to steal it back. But the guy was super fast and I was at least ten feet behind him when he took a shot.

That was when I realized that it was the camper who'd

pushed past me and Russ on our way to the dorm. The guy I'd called a jerk.

I watched his shot fly through the air and into the basket. *Swish.*

The crowd cheered and all I could think about was making them shout and clap for *me.*

Get back in the game, O.

The other guard passed me the ball, and I dribbled down the court again.

"Over here," one of the guys shouted. I waited for a second or two more before deciding to hand it off.

Big mistake.

The Jerk popped up right in front of me. He blocked the pass, snatched the ball, and took off for the net.

Again.

Nuts!

I should have joined the Reds.

He passed the ball to an open player, who scored. Of course.

On the way back down the court, someone tapped me on the shoulder. I turned to see the kid who'd been next to me on the bench.

"I'm subbing in," he said.

"What? You mean for me?"

"Yeah."

"But I haven't had a chance to do anything yet."

"Believe me," the kid said. "You've done enough."

"But—"

"Back to the bench, Showboat."

"I'm not a—"

"Come on. You're holding up the game."

I looked around and saw that he was right. No one was moving and the only sound on the court was the ball slapping the hardwood as the other guard bounced it and stared at me.

I walked off the court and sat down on the bench with a *thud*. "That's not even fair," I muttered. "I was barely even out there."

"Don't worry about it," the curly-haired kid next to me said. "We've got a whole week to play."

"I guess," I said, with a sigh, noticing his Farina jersey.

Farina was an awesome player, but who would wear a *Lakers* jersey to a camp in *Oregon*?

"I'm Jackson," he said.

He stuck out a hand for me to shake, which nobody our age did, but I shook it, anyway. "Owen."

"Nice to meet you."

"Yeah." I nodded, turning to watch the game. And watching was all I got to do for the next fifteen minutes.

It was a total drag.

"Orientation starts pretty soon," Jackson said. "Do you want to head over there with me?"

I glanced at him. "You don't want to get some playing time in?"

"Like I said, we've got a whole week. And I'd like a good seat."

I thought about that for a second. It wouldn't hurt to be front and center, where the coaches would see me and know I was a go-getter.

"Okay, let's roll," I said, pulling my T-shirt back on. I followed Jackson through the main doors and into the courtyard. "Where are you from?" I asked, just to make conversation.

"LA."

"Like, California?" I gasped.

He laughed. "Is there another LA?"

"No, but you came all the way up here for Hoopsters?"

Jackson nodded. "My dad knows one of the owners and he invited me to come."

"That's so cool," I said, totally jealous.

Jackson shrugged and was quiet until we got to Gym One. He pulled open the heavy door and I followed him inside.

Just like Freeman Court, the place was awesome. A microphone and a bunch of chairs were set up on a volleyball court in the center of the building. I saw a sign in the shape of an arrow, pointing toward a swimming pool. Other signs pointed to a weight room, locker rooms, and an indoor track.

"Whoa," I said, taking it all in. "Nice."

"Yeah," Jackson said, walking right past a table filled with all kinds of energy bars, fruit, and bottles of water and juice.

My stomach growled.

"How about these seats?" Jackson asked, pointing to the back corner.

"I was thinking up front," I told him, starting down the aisle. "So they know we're serious."

"Oh," he said, sounding kind of disappointed. "Okay."

I chose a prime spot at dead center in the first row and we sat down to wait for the rest of the Hoopsters to show up.

"Bright and early," a man said, appearing out of nowhere and walking toward the microphone. He was wearing a Hoopsters cap and carrying a clipboard, so I knew he was important.

"We don't want to miss anything," I told him, sitting up straight.

He smiled. "I like it. You boys are ready."

I grinned back, knowing I didn't need Orientation.

I'd already found my place at the head of the class.

Theoretical Probability

When I looked up from my reading to check the clock, I saw that I had only a few minutes to spare before the Multisport Orientation.

How had the time slipped away so quickly?

Oh, yeah. I'd been enjoying myself.

I reluctantly tucked a bookmark into position and changed into shorts and a T-shirt. I double knotted my shoes without the usual reminder from Owen.

The dorm was absolutely still as I made my way downstairs, which meant there was no one to ask for directions. Not even Owen, who was already busy with an Orientation session of his own.

I remembered the campus map included in my welcome packet and breathed a sigh of relief.

When I made it safely to the gym, I discovered it was buzzing with activity. I found a table loaded with name tags and other paraphernalia, so I carefully filled out a tag and made a check mark next to my name on the registration list.

"This is going to be so cool!" the guy behind me blurted when I passed him the pen.

"What is?" I asked.

"Uh, Multisport camp?" he said, like it was the most obvious thing in the world.

"You *wanted* to come to this one?" I asked, stunned.

He looked at me like I'd lost my mind. "Well, I didn't want to spend a whole week playing just baseball or basketball or whatever."

"You didn't?"

"Nah. I already do that in gym class."

He had a point. "Sure, but—"

"I mean, we get to do *pole vaulting here*. How cool is that?"

How *cool*?

It was lukewarm, at best.

Never mind *terrifying.*

When I didn't say anything, he shrugged. "See you around."

"Sure," I said as he walked away.

"Man, I'm so glad we get to play soccer this year," I heard someone behind me say.

"Pretty awesome," another voice agreed. "Remember how much fun football was last time?"

"*You* liked football," the first guy said. "I liked swimming."

"Did I tell you that when my brother came a couple of years ago they had karate?"

"Sweet! Maybe it'll be back next year."

Excitement continued to fill the air around me and I wished I could gather some enthusiasm of my own.

Most of the rows were filled with kids, but I found a seat near the back and took it.

If I'd been attending a class, I would have been disappointed by the poor location, but Multisport Sampler camp was something else entirely. Disappearing at the rear of the crowd suited me perfectly.

The redheaded boy sitting on my left offered me a piece of gum when I sat down. I took one, hoping it wasn't some kind of a hint about my breath.

"I can't believe I'm actually here," he said, grinning.

I sighed. "Neither can I."

Apparently, my tone was lost on him and the dark clouds of doom above my head were not visible to the naked eye. He actually raised his hand for a high five.

Sighing again, I gave him one.

While I waited for Orientation to begin, I took the time to study my surroundings. The building was architecturally beautiful and filled with a natural glow from countless skylights in the ceiling.

It would have been the perfect place to sit and read.

"Welcome, campers!" a voice boomed from the front of the room.

An assortment of adults stood shoulder to shoulder in front of the crowd, all wearing camp hats. Their smiles were as big and bright as the ones I saw on the faces of every camper.

Every camper but one, anyway.

I took a deep breath, then muttered, "And so it begins."

"What?" the boy next to me whispered.

"Nothing," I told him.

For the next twenty minutes, I listened to earnest talk about stretching our limits, trying new things, and having "a blast" doing it. Again, I wished the energy was contagious, but all I could think about was how many minutes were left before soccer began.

How many minutes of anonymity could I enjoy before everyone at camp found out that I didn't belong there?

As the adults addressed the group, I wished for at least the tenth time that I'd stood up to Owen and demanded the Hoopsters spot, if only for the sake of it being a familiar sport. Of course, I knew that basketball wouldn't have solved anything for me. Putting a big orange ball through a hoop wouldn't erase my total and utter failure at state.

Nothing would.

The truth was, I'd come to the horrible conclusion that my Masters of the Mind career was over. The team needed someone who would come through for them when it counted.

They deserved better.

"So," the final speaker continued, "I know you'll all be excited to hear that on Friday we have a very special event planned."

My hopes lifted for a moment, at the thought of a day of rest and recovery, but in my heart I knew that wasn't going to happen.

"We'll be staging a sort of mini-Olympics, where you'll compete in all of the sports we cover this week. Parents are invited to attend." He smiled. "And we'll even have a medal ceremony."

The buzz of excitement grew even louder.

"You'll be split into four teams before you leave this building and those teams will be yours for the week. It's up to you to come up with team names."

"Awesome," the kid next to me whispered.

That was debatable.

Then again, choosing a name would likely be the only creative moment I experienced all week.

That was as close to awesome as it might get.

I barely heard the last few remarks made by the staff and the next thing I knew, Orientation was over. When I stood up, I was immediately swept up in the current of campers.

I knew from my schedule that teams A though D would rotate through sessions in soccer, volleyball, and track and field in turn.

I had no idea how my week would play out, so I took a

deep breath and followed the arrows to the indoor arena, bracing myself for disaster.

✖   ÷   ✚

When my fellow C Team members and I lined up on the field, a coach who introduced himself as Hernandez blew his whistle to end the chatter.

"Okay, folks," he said when we'd all quieted down, "let's start with some stretching and a couple of laps around the field to warm up."

Here we go.

I rolled my shoulders, trying to eliminate some of the tension I'd been carrying around since state. I followed Coach's lead as he ran us through a series of stretches, relieved that several of them were exactly what the Pioneers did at practice. At least that much was familiar.

Unfortunately, the only other familiar component was running.

C Team took off in a solid pack, but it only took a few strides before a number of my teammates bolted ahead.

"This isn't a race," Coach Hernandez shouted after them and I gasped with relief until he added, "The racing comes later!"

I tried to find my own pace and ignore the fact that so many people were passing me. I should have just started at the back.

Step, step, inhale.

Step, step, exhale.

The turf felt strange under my feet and I couldn't help noticing the resistance it created. It was actually more work to run on the field than on the court, which wasn't exactly a delightful discovery.

I kept my elbows bent, like Owen had shown me, and tried to think of anything to distract me from the task at hand. Of course, my inclination was toward the periodic table.

Nonmetals. Hydrogen, nitrogen, carbon, oxygen.

I got stuck on oxygen. I needed some. Desperately.

"Take it easy," Coach Hernandez said, appearing next to me and matching my pace. "You don't want to hurt yourself."

He was absolutely right about that.

Step, step, inhale.

Step, step, exhale.

"Do you need to stop?" he asked, sounding concerned.

Did I *want* to stop? Absolutely.

But *need* to?

It was only day one.

I thought about the running I'd done to prepare for Pioneer tryouts and how every breath felt like it would be my last. I thought about running lines and hating every second of it. Missing the basket more times than I could count.

Then I thought about how good it felt to make the team.

All of the pain had been worth it.

I took a ragged breath. "I'm okay," I told him.

"Good job," he said, slapping me on the back as he picked up the pace to catch up to the guys ahead of me.

I let the words echo in my mind.

Good job. Good job. Good job.

By the time I finished my second lap, I felt tired but satisfied. I may not have been the fastest kid out there, but I did it.

When the agony was over, I tried to catch my breath and noticed I wasn't the only one who needed a moment. Two of the guys had adopted the stance of the exhausted, hands on their knees as they sucked in precious air. Another was walking it off, his carefully spiked hair already wilting.

Coach blew his whistle. "Nice work, everyone. Now, I'm going to split you up into four smaller teams to scrimmage."

He started at the left side of the crowd and made us count off, one through four. I was a three, so I moved to my designated area and joined the group.

"I usually play striker," the redhead who sat next to me at Orientation said.

Striker?

What on earth was that?

"I'm a defender," another said.

"Me, too, but I can play halfback if we need one."

It sounded like too many positions. Too many players. I'd thought that, aside from the goalkeeper, soccer was like basketball, with three forwards and two guards.

I turned to the guy next to me. "How many players are on the field at a time?"

"Eleven," he said, looking at me like I'd lost my mind.

"*Eleven?*"

"Yeah," he said, nodding. "Unless you're playing with six-year-olds."

I probably should have been.

"Oh," I said, then confided, "I've never played before."

"What?" he gasped.

"What's going on?" the curly-haired kid next to him asked.

"He's never played *soccer*." His tone hinted that the fact was as bizarre as never drawing a breath.

"Who?" One of the others asked.

"This guy."

"No way."

I could feel the heat of embarrassment in my cheeks.

Phosphorus, sulphur . . .

"That's impossible."

"Where's he from?" a kid in a baseball cap asked.

"Okay, I'm right here," I reminded them, feeling exasperated.

"Yeah, but where are you *from*?"

"Portland," I told the group.

"You've never heard of the Timbers?" he asked.

"They're only my favorite soccer team," the curly-haired one said.

"Football Club, not soccer team," the redhead corrected. "Portland Timbers Football Club."

"Why are you telling *him*?" the guy next to me asked. "This beanpole's the one who's never heard of them."

"I didn't say I'd never *heard of*—" Wait. *Beanpole*?

"I can't believe you've never played," Baseball Cap said, shaking his head.

I'd had enough. "I've played kickball in gym class."

The entire group fell silent, aside from the guy next to me who slapped his forehead. "You're killing me, man."

A whistle blew a few yards behind us. "Let's go, folks!" Coach Hernandez shouted, tossing our group a handful of red vests.

I hurriedly put mine on, getting tangled up in the process, and ran onto the field with the rest of the guys. They all seemed to know exactly where to go, and if two players ended up in the same position, they quickly adjusted.

"Where am I supposed to be?" I asked Baseball Cap.

He scanned the field. "Be a midfielder, I guess." He glanced back at me and must have been able to tell I had no idea what that was. "That means you're at *midfield*," he said, pointing.

I ran into what I hoped was the right area and when Coach Hernandez blew his whistle to start the scrimmage, I ran in the general direction of the ball, hoping I wouldn't actually reach it.

Almost immediately, it was kicked directly at me and I did the only thing that came naturally.

I caught it.

Coach Hernandez's whistle could barely be heard over the shouts of my teammates.

"Okay, okay," he said, waving his arms until they quieted down. "Not everyone here has the same level of experience." His stern gaze moved from one face to the next until he got to me. "So, the first rule of soccer is—"

"*No hands!*" everyone yelled at once.

After the scrimmage, which was easily the most confusing twenty minutes of my life, Coach directed our attention to the straight lines of orange cones at the end of the field.

The formation looked exactly like what the Pioneers used to practice dribbling.

The nightmare continues.

We stayed in our four groups and lined up behind the cones, awaiting Coach's whistle. My palms sweated as I considered the fact that in a matter of seconds, everyone would be reminded of exactly how terrible I was.

At the blast of the whistle, the first boys took off, tapping their soccer balls with the toes and sides of their shoes. The redhead moved with amazing speed and agility, but I was relieved when others stumbled as they turned to make their way back.

As each new batch of players took off, my heart pounded

a little faster. I wiped the sweat from my hands onto my shorts and waited for my turn, wishing I was somewhere else.

Anywhere else.

"Are you ready?" the redhead asked.

"I hope so."

When I was finally at the front of the line, the ball was passed to me, but it went straight through my legs. I chased after it and started to carry it back to the first cone.

A loud blast of the whistle let me know that was incorrect.

"No hands," Coach Hernandez shouted. "Feet only, please."

I felt the heat in my cheeks and knew I was blushing. I quickly dropped the ball and tapped it with my toe. But I didn't use enough force and when I took a step to jog after it, I tripped over it instead.

"Whoa," one of the guys said. "Fancy footwork."

"He stinks," a voice I recognized as Baseball Cap's added.

I could tell by the murmuring that followed that most of the boys agreed with him.

There was nothing in the world I wanted more than to leave the ball (and the entire sport of soccer) where it lay and run back to the dorm to read.

But that wasn't an option.

I tried dribbling again, only this time I kicked the ball too hard and it shot past my first two cones.

"Are you kidding me?" one of the boys exclaimed.

"Well?" Coach Hernandez called out to me. "Catch up with it."

I took a deep breath and ran after the ball, feeling just as clumsy and out of place as the day I tried out for the Pioneers.

Of course, I was well aware that basketball had worked out for me. By fluke, I had some natural ability and a lot of practicing had helped me to become an important part of the team. But, statistically speaking, I knew that the chance of me having natural ability in another sport was about as likely as being struck by lightning.

Twice.

No, this camp was going to be a series of failures, one after another.

Just as I reached the ball, Coach Hernandez appeared next to me. "Nice and gentle," he said.

I glanced at him and when I saw that he was being sincere, I softly tapped the ball with my toe.

"Perfect," Coach said. "Now use the other foot. Just nudge it back and forth to guide it."

"I've never done this before," I admitted.

"I noticed," Coach said.

I looked at him, mortified. "I'm sorry, it's just—"

"There's a first time for everything," he interrupted. "You've got to work your way through every cone. Just take it as slow as you need to."

That turned out to be slower than anyone could have imagined.

By the time I reached the end of the cones, every other group was finished. And that meant that I had the attention of everyone on the field.

"Keep going," Coach said, walking next to me. "It's getting better."

That was entirely untrue, but I appreciated him saying it.

"What's your name?"

"Russell," I told him.

"Okay, Russell. You're already halfway there."

I inched around the final cone, one awkward tap at a time until I was facing the rest of the kids.

"Let's give Russell some help, boys," Coach called to them.

To my great surprise, I heard someone shout, "You can do it!"

I looked up and saw that it was the redhead. He gave me a thumbs-up.

"It's the final stretch," another voice called.

I concentrated on using just enough force to move the ball in a controlled manner. I glanced upward. Only eight cones stood between me and the end of the drill.

I could handle eight cones.

"Now, you've got it," Coach said, staying with me.

I tapped the ball again and only bumped the first cone once as I made my way past it.

"Nice!" someone shouted.

The next cone was easier, and soon enough I had a rhythm

going. It might have been an extremely slow and awkward rhythm, but it was something.

By the time I made it past the final cone, I had easily taken three times longer than anyone else. I was sweaty, embarrassed, and still wishing I was back in my room.

Then Coach said something that surprised me.

"That, boys, was a lesson not just in soccer, but in life."

It was?

"What you just witnessed," he continued, "was a perfect example of persistence. Russell just showed all of us what it means to stick to it, to keep trying when it seems impossible. To not give up." He paused. "Let's give him a round of applause."

I couldn't help smiling when the clapping began.

Out-of-Bounds

I was totally psyched about Orientation.

They handed out our T-shirts, which were cool, even though they were gray instead of a flashier color. They said HOOPSTERS on the front and that was the most important thing, anyway. They also gave us stopwatches that we could use to time ourselves running and as alarm clocks in the morning.

Ha! As if I'd need an *alarm clock* to wake me up during the most awesome week of my life! I was pretty sure my body would jolt awake every morning, no problem.

Then, at the very end, they told us something awesome.

"On Friday, there will be a round-robin tournament your parents are invited to attend. There will also be a special surprise guest joining us. And that guest will present the MVP award."

"Special guest?" I asked as the crowd left their seats, but Jackson didn't hear me.

"Usually it's a pro," the guy behind me said.

I spun around to face him. "An NBA pro?"

"Uh, *yeah*," he said, like that was obvious.

"I wonder who it is," I said, starting to get excited.

What if it was Carl Walters? He was having his best Blazers season ever! Or maybe Kevin Maple? Lamar Otis? Could we ask for autographs? No, wait, if Mom and Dad were there, they could take a picture of me with whoever the guest was.

That would be even better than an autograph.

My brain was filling up with ideas about who the pro would be when I joined the rest of the guys to load up on juice and snacks.

Hands full, we all headed over to Freeman Court, where Hoopsters would officially get rolling.

I couldn't wait!

There were eight head coaches, so we were split up into eight teams. I didn't get to choose which one I was on, but I got lucky and ended up with Coach Phillips, who I'd met at Orientation.

The unlucky part was that one of my teammates was the Jerk.

And even worse than that? He was a freakishly awesome player.

The session started with running a few laps, which was cool until the Jerk (who turned out to be called Big Mike) passed me and made some snotty comment I didn't catch.

Then we did some of the drills Coach Baxter ran us through back home, which meant I was in my comfort zone. While we practiced dribbling around cones and all of the usual stuff, I tried to ignore how smooth and fast some of the guys were. I knew the campers were all under fourteen, but some of them played like grown men.

I stared at Big Mike.

And looked like them!

I concentrated on keeping control of the ball, figuring that even if I wasn't the fastest guy out there, Coach would at least see my solid ball-handling skills.

But when I looked around, it was obvious that everyone was skilled.

Seriously skilled.

I'd kind of expected to make a splash right off the bat, but the competition was fierce.

Or maybe I just hadn't had my chance yet.

"Okay, boys," Coach Phillips said. "I want you to split up into pairs for some one-on-one."

"Hey, Owen," Jackson said, tapping me on the back. "Want to be my partner?"

I hadn't even noticed he was on my team.

I thought about it for a moment. I would have liked to be paired off with one of the good players, so I could prove myself. Then again, if I played one-on-one against Jackson, I'd probably look even better.

"Uh, sure," I said, following him to one of the baskets.

"Want to start?" he asked, offering me the ball.

Offense was my thing, so the more time I spent lining up shots, the better. "Sure," I said, dribbling the ball a couple of times, then bouncing it between my legs, just in case anyone was looking.

"Nice," Jackson said, but didn't make a move toward me. I still couldn't get over the Lakers jersey. Blazers gear would have made way more sense.

"Ready?" I asked, bouncing the ball back and forth, from one hand to the other.

He shrugged. "I guess so."

I waited for him to take a step, but he didn't even move. My one-on-one was more like one-on-zero. Well, I didn't have all day to mess around. I faked left and went right, making an easy layup.

"That's two for me," I said, tossing him the ball.

"Want another try?"

"You don't want to shoot?" I asked, totally surprised.

"It doesn't matter."

I stared at him. "This is Hoopsters, Jackson. You're supposed to shoot."

"I know, but it's fine with me if you want to."

I wasn't about to turn down the first chance I'd really had to shine. I caught the ball he passed back to me, happy to be his partner. The kid was making me look as good as Russ did.

Maybe even better.

I dribbled the ball in, trying to throw Jackson off by looking to one side, then the other. I was being super careful to make sure he couldn't tell which way I was going, but it didn't matter. His feet stayed planted on the ground.

I scored another basket with a nice loud *swish*.

"Are those Adidas made of concrete or something?" I joked as I dribbled back to the line, ready to take another run at the net.

Jackson looked at his feet and laughed. "Nope."

"Want to try to steal the ball from me this time?"

He shrugged. "I thought you wanted to score."

What was the deal with this kid?

"Of course I want to score, but this is supposed to be one-on-one."

"Okay," Jackson said. He lifted his hands and waved them in the air, like he was flagging down a bus.

"Seriously?" I asked.

"What?"

"That's how you're covering me?"

"What's wrong with it?" he asked.

Instead of telling him why it wouldn't work, I showed him. I zipped around him, dodged his arms, and made another basket. "That's two more."

MVP, here I come.

After a few minutes and eight more points for me, Coach made us rotate to new partners.

This time, I was matched up with that kid Tyrelle I'd seen tearing it up before camp even started.

"Hey," he said. "I'm T. J."

"Owen," I told him as we bumped fists.

He sniffed a couple of times, like he smelled something bad.

"What?" I asked, taking a whiff.

"What what?" he asked, looking like I'd insulted him.

"You just—"

"Are you ready to play?" he asked, then sniffed again.

I inhaled, but couldn't smell anything!

Was he trying to psych me out?

I had the ball but wished he was the one dribbling so I could see what I was up against. Instead, I watched him closely as I dribbled, trying to keep an eye on every move he made, from where his toes pointed to which hand seemed most ready to make a grab for the ball.

What I hadn't counted on was his eye contact. It was like we were stuck in a staring contest and neither one of us would blink.

At least I could focus on something other than the sniffing.

At the exact moment I glanced toward the basket, he knew I was making my move and he sprung into action.

In half a second, he had one hand on the ball, and by the time the second passed, he'd stolen it.

"What was that?" I demanded when he scored his two points.

"Basketball," he said, smiling.

"No, you hypnotized me or something."

"I *what*?" he asked as the smile turned into a laugh.

"You did . . . something to me. You got me all messed up."

He bounced the ball a couple of times and sniffed again. "The point of the drill is to score, Owen."

"I know. It's just—"

"It's just you weren't the one to do it."

"No. You did some weird thing with your eyes and . . . never mind," I snapped.

"Okay," he said, bouncing the ball again. "Are you ready to guard me?"

"Yeah," I said, hoping I was right.

The next thing I knew, he had whipped past me and scored another basket.

"Come on!"

"What? I asked if you were ready and you said yes."

"I know, but—"

"But what?" he asked, tucking the ball under his arm.

"You didn't even look at me before you took off."

He shook his head. "Last time you complained that I *did* look at you."

I felt like I was on a debate team or something.

Luckily, Coach blew his whistle and it was time for us to rotate again.

I was relieved until I turned around.

Aw, man!

I should have known I'd get stuck with Big Mike.

"Hey," I said, nodding at him. He didn't say anything back, so I knew I was right about him being a jerk. "I'm Owen."

He picked the ball up from the floor and said, "Everybody calls you Samsonite."

I stared at him, totally confused. "What?"

"You're the kid who can't lift his own suitcase." He smirked as he bounced the ball once on the hardwood. "They should be calling you Samson-lite."

"Very funny," I muttered.

"*I* think so." Two more bounces.

"Are we playing, or what?" I asked. I wanted my chance to show my stuff and this guy was wasting time. Eating the clock.

"Ooh, tough guy," he said, laughing.

"I'm here for the basketball, okay?"

He looked me over from head to toe. "Sure. But just remember you asked for it."

"Asked for—" I started, but he faked me out and went in for a layup before I got the last word out.

"How do you like me now?" he teased, throwing me a bounce pass.

I don't.

I took a moment to dribble in place, trying to get some kind of a rhythm going. The last thing I needed was for Big Mike to psych me out, but it was already too late.

"Are we playing, or what?" he asked, mimicking me.

I gritted my teeth, bounced the ball one more time, and went for it. I made it two steps and was aiming for a shot when he blocked me completely. He was so big, he didn't even have to use his arms. He was a wall and I couldn't even see the hoop.

I tried to pivot, so I could get my back to him, but he snatched the ball before I could. I jumped to get it back, but it was way out of reach. The next thing I knew, his shot was bouncing off the backboard and right in the basket.

Great.

This guy would totally steal my thunder at Friday's tournament!

Big Mike smiled at me as he dribbled the ball back and forth again, from one hand to the other, never taking his eyes off mine. "Maybe volleyball camp is more your speed."

I shot him a dirty look, and he laughed.

As much as I wanted to run at him and grab the ball, I waited, knees bent, arms out, ready to move in whatever direction he did.

He came toward me slowly and just as I lunged for the ball, he spun around and I got nothing but back. I lost my balance and fell over, hitting the floor at the exact same time the ball hit the backboard.

It went on like that for another few minutes, until Coach finally blew the whistle and we rotated again.

I had better luck with the next guy, but never really got going.

By the time we broke for lunch, I was happy to walk away from Freeman Court.

All I could think about on the way to the cafeteria was how mad I was that there were players as awesome as Big Mike and T. J. at camp. *I* wanted to be the star player, the guy who rocked the hardwood all week and got the MVP award.

But how was I supposed to do that when I was surrounded by hotshots?

When I walked into the cafeteria, I was ready to dodge Jackson if I saw him. He was nice and everything, but he wasn't like those other guys. And between the Lakers gear and his lack of skills on the court, he definitely wasn't someone I wanted to be stuck with all week.

I picked up a ham sandwich, an apple, and a bottle of chocolate milk, then headed into the seating area. I hadn't thought about the fact that every camp would be breaking around the same time. There were a ton of guys in the noisy room, and it looked like practically every table was full.

I felt like a total dork, standing there, holding my tray and hoping someone would invite me to sit down.

No one did.

Luckily, I spotted my brother's curly head bobbing down one of the aisles.

Sitting with a nerd who was mad at me was better than sitting by myself.

"Russ!" I shouted.

He stopped and turned around. He had a bottle of orange juice in one hand and a paper bag in the other.

"What's in the bag?" I asked when I caught up with him.

"A sandwich and a couple of cookies."

I looked around. "Where were the cookies?"

"Next to the cooler. Peanut butter or chocolate chip."

"Cool," I said, starting to go back for some. "Save me a seat. I'll be right behind you."

"I'm not staying."

What?

I spun around, and he held up the paper bag. "I'm heading back to my room."

I hurried over to him. "You're going to eat lunch in your room? Why?"

He shrugged. "I want to get a little reading in."

"Seriously? Russ, this is the chance of a lifetime, and you're going to waste it, sitting by yourself with your nose buried in a book?"

He gave me a long look. "Yes." He started to walk away.

"Russ! Just come eat with me."

Instead of turning around, he held one hand up in the air in a backward good-bye.

"Who was that?" Jackson asked.

I hadn't even heard him sneak up on me!

I sighed. "My twin brother."

Jackson looked confused. "Your twin—"

"Fraternal," I said, before he could finish the question everyone asked when they saw us together.

We carried our trays down one aisle then another and I scanned the room for a spot to sit. Most of the guys we passed already looked like best friends.

Like they'd known each other forever.

Suddenly, I found myself missing all of my buddies from the Pioneers. We were a team on the court *and* off. We sat by each other in classes and hung out in the cafeteria at lunch. We were a tight unit. Without those guys, I felt . . . lonely.

And Russ was no help.

At all.

How long could that guy carry a grudge, anyway? It had to get heavy at some point, just like my Samsonite.

Didn't it?

"There's a table," Jackson said, tilting his head toward the back corner.

"Cool," I said, even though it wasn't.

In fact, nothing at Hoopsters was as cool as I thought it would be.

I thought about that for a moment and realized it wasn't totally true. The courts were cool, the coaches were cool, and I had to admit the other kids were cool, too.

I guess *I* was the only thing at camp that wasn't as cool as I thought it would be.

I swallowed hard.

Things had to turn around fast if I was going to get everything out of Hoopsters that I wanted to.

Exponential Growth

It seemed like I'd barely sat down to read before it was time for the next soccer session. I slipped my shoes back on before rolling off the bed and heading for the door.

I'd ended the first session on a surprisingly high note and hoped the trend would continue.

As I reached for the doorknob, I heard someone turning it from outside. When the door swung open, I was facing Danny.

"Oh, hey, Russ," he said, grinning as he passed me on his way into the room. "I'm just grabbing my old shoes. These ones aren't worn in and they're giving me blisters."

"Blisters are the worst," I agreed.

"Hey, I didn't see you in the cafeteria."

"I uh . . . ate in here."

Danny frowned. "Why?"

I wanted to be as tactful as possible about the fact that I was dreading an entire week of shared accommodations and that I was someone who needed ample time alone.

I pointed to the novel I'd been reluctant to leave behind. "So I could read and—"

"That must be a pretty awesome book," he said.

"It is," I told him, feeling a smile fill my face. "It's the latest in a series about an alien culture living on—"

Danny held up a hand to stop me. "I'm not really into sci-fi."

"Oh, well it would actually be better categorized as fantasy," I started to explain, but could tell by the expression on his face that it wasn't helping.

Danny slipped off his shoes and left them in the middle of the floor, in a move reminiscent of Owen. Then he pulled another pair out of his gym bag and sat down on the edge of the bed. *My bed*.

Terrific.

On top of being a social butterfly, he was a space invader.

After he'd tied the first bow, he looked up at me and said, "So, T. J. noticed you . . . noticing him."

"What?"

"You know, the nose thing." He raised his eyebrows in a question.

"The nose thing," I repeated, thinking of that constant sniffing.

"He has a tic, Russ."

I winced. *I should have realized that's what it was.* "Oh. I didn't mean to stare."

"It's okay. I'm just telling you so you know. It only happens when he's nervous or uncomfortable."

"He sniffs," I said, nodding.

"Yeah. Some people sniff, some people blink or clear their throats . . . and some people reach for a book."

What?

I looked at the novel in my hands and felt my cheeks get hot. "I wasn't—"

"Geez, I'm *kidding*, Russ," he said, chuckling. "Anyway, once he gets used to you, it'll stop. Just try not to stare in the meantime, okay?"

"Absolutely," I said, embarrassed that I'd already done it.

"So, if you're interested, me and some of the guys are putting together some pranks for tonight—"

"Pranks?"

"Yeah, short-sheeting beds and stuff like that."

"Uh . . ."

He raised an eyebrow at me. "You don't know what that is?"

"No," I admitted.

"It's when you sneak into someone's room and you take the flat sheet on their bed and tuck it in at the head instead of at the feet," he explained, excitedly. "Then you fold it in half, so when the guy gets into bed, his legs get jammed up."

I stared at him. "But . . . *why?*"

He laughed. "Because he won't know what's wrong, and the look of surprise on his face—"

"You stay in the room?" I asked.

"What? No, but—"

"And isn't it dark, anyway? How can you see the look of surprise?"

Danny looked somewhat deflated. "It's more about the morning after, when everyone's talking about it."

I seriously doubted I'd tell anyone if I got "jammed up" in my bed due to sabotaged sheets.

"Anyway," Danny continued, not to be deterred. "We thought we'd get the guy next door. You know, the one with the suitcase and the attitude."

"Owen," I said quietly. I felt like my entire body was wincing.

"Yeah. The one you met on the stairs. Big Mike told me about how he was holding everybody up."

It wasn't the first time in my life I'd been tempted to pretend that I didn't know my own brother. But, like every other occasion, I couldn't bring myself to do it.

"Uh, we didn't actually *meet* there," I told him, adjusting my glasses. I took a deep breath and confessed, "He's my twin brother."

Danny howled with laughter. "Now *that* is hilarious."

"What?" I asked, stunned. It was a reaction I'd never come across before.

"Russ, you've got to say that to Big Mike when he comes over later."

"I'm serious," I told him.

He laughed even harder. "That you're *twins*."

"We are. Fraternal twins." I paused for a second. "Look, I know you guys want to have fun, but could you please leave Owen out of it?"

He stopped laughing and tilted his head at me. "Hold on. You really *are* serious, aren't you?"

"Yes."

He shook his head. "But if you're brothers, why aren't you sharing a room?"

I explained the whole situation as concisely as I could, trying not to make Owen sound like a total jerk.

"Huh," Danny said when I was finished. "So, he snagged the better room *and* the better camp."

Apparently I'd failed on the jerk front.

"Yes."

Danny was quiet for a moment, then said, "I know the guys will want to mess with him a bit, just because of, you know . . . the way he is."

"I know." I sighed.

"But I'll try to keep him out of it."

Surprised, I choked, "Really? Thank you!"

Danny shrugged. "No problem," he said, tying the other shoe and standing. "I'll catch you later, Russ."

"Yeah," I said, smiling. "Definitely."

✕   ÷   ✚

I was feeling better than I had in weeks when I headed to my second soccer session. And when I arrived, I was immediately welcomed by Coach Hernandez.

"Good break?" he asked, moving to stand next to me.

"Absolutely," I told him.

"I've got some plans for you, Russ."

"Plans?"

"I'm going to try you out in goal." He paused. "You're focused, you've got a good reach . . . and, other than throwins, goaltending is the only time you get to use your hands in this sport."

I cringed a little, remembering my catch during that first scrimmage.

"How does that sound?" he asked.

"Good," I told him, glad that he saw some potential in me.

"Great," he said, slapping me on the back. "We'll get you into position for this next drill."

Smiling to myself, I made my way over to the goal.

He was right.

I *was* focused.

I *did* have a good reach.

It was quite possible that goal could be the perfect spot for me. And the added bonus? It didn't require running.

Assistant Coach Baylor gave me a long-sleeved yellow jersey to wear over my T-shirt, along with a pair of gloves with bumpy grips.

I stepped past one of the white posts and into the goal. The first thing I noticed was that the distance to the other post was a lot greater than I'd expected.

Hmm.

I walked from one end to the other, surprised by how many steps it took.

The area I was expected to cover was . . . huge.

"Have you played goalie before?" Baylor asked.

I shook my head. "Never."

"How about I give you a couple of pointers?"

"That would be excellent," I said, relieved.

"When they're coming toward you, you'll want to get in a crouch, like this," he said, bending his knees while keeping his legs apart.

"Like a guarding position in basketball."

"Very close," Coach Baylor said, nodding. "You want to be able to spring in either direction quickly."

"That makes sense."

"Different goalies have different styles, but I like bent elbows, hands up and ready."

I nodded, mimicking his stance. I wondered whether I looked like a mime in a box and sort of chuckled.

"There we go," Coach Baylor said. "That's the first smile I've seen you crack all day." He paused. "Camp is supposed to be fun, you know."

"I know," I told him.

A lot of things were supposed to be . . . a lot of things.

For example, my Masters of the Mind team was supposed to be on our way to nationals.

I shook my head to clear the thought away. I needed to concentrate on the positive.

"Are you ready?" Coach Baylor asked.

"Sure," I told him.

But I was dead wrong.

Coach Hernandez blew his whistle and all of the other guys formed two lines, one to my right and one to my left. Each of the boys in front had a ball and the assistant coaches were standing by, holding mesh bags filled with more.

"Okay!" Coach Hernandez shouted. "At my whistle, we start on the left and alternate."

Alternate what?

I found out soon enough, when the sound of the whistle pierced the air and the first guy in line dribbled toward me.

I got into position, hands up and ready to catch the ball.

The player was moving awfully fast.

How was I going to—

The ball flew passed me at a tremendous speed.

Stunned, I turned around to see it tangled in the back corner of the net. I heard another whistle blast, but by the time I turned back around, another ball was racing toward my face.

I jumped out of the way, tripping over my feet in the process.

Bweep!

Another ball came out of nowhere, this one hitting me in the chest with much more force than expected.

"Nice block!" Coach Baylor shouted.

"Block?" I choked.

Bweep!

Another ball rocketed toward me. I lifted my elbow to shield my face and it bounced off my funny bone.

"Use your hands," Coach Hernandez called out to me.

I was tempted to raise them in surrender.

Bweep!

The redhead took his shot, and I felt a light breeze through my hair as the ball missed my ear by inches.

"Hold on," I said, but no one was listening.

Bweep!

"Hey," I said a bit louder as another player took aim.

When yet another ball came right at me, I turned away and felt it pound against my back.

"*Time-out!*" Coach Baylor shouted.

Of course. *That* was the word I'd been searching for.

"What's the problem?" Coach Hernandez asked, meeting Coach Baylor a few feet away from me.

"Russ, you've got to go for the ball," Baylor said.

"But the ball's going for *me*," I explained, "like a guided missile."

"I thought you wanted to try goal," Coach Hernandez said, looking disappointed.

"I did. I mean, I *do*."

"Then let's give it another shot," he said.

"Great," I muttered as he walked away. "More shots."

I sighed as I adjusted my glasses. The mud from my gloves smeared the lenses, but I didn't have time to clean them off.

Bweep!

The next ball was coming in way above my head.

"Jump for it!" Coach Baylor shouted.

I leaped into the air, arms stretched as far as they would go, but my fingertips barely grazed the ball.

"Nice effort!" Baylor called out to me.

I took a deep breath, reminding myself that nothing is easy the first time.

Except maybe algebraic equations.

Bweep!

And calculating atomic weight.

This time, I watched closely as the player dribbled, trying to figure out what he was going to do before he actually did it.

To my surprise, I noticed that he leaned *left* just before he took the shot with his *right* foot.

Aha!

I took a couple of steps, anticipating the ball. I raised my hands to chest level, and when it came toward me, I actually caught it.

I barely felt the sting in my hands as Coach Hernandez shouted, "Nice save!"

Astonished by my success, I was tempted to take a bow, but a whistle blast brought me back to my senses.

$$\times \quad \div \quad +$$

At dinner that night, I grabbed a sandwich to take back to the room. After a rather exhausting but satisfying day of soccer, I couldn't wait to relax with my book.

To my surprise, when I was on my way through the cafeteria, heading for the exit, I was invited to sit at a couple of different tables.

"Come on, Russ," the redhead I'd learned was Sam urged. "We're trying to come up with our team name."

That was intriguing enough to pull me in.

"What have you come up with so far?" I asked as I stood at the end of the table.

"Nothing," my teammate James said. "We're the C team, so we figured it should start with a C."

"*Hmm.*" I thought about it for a moment. "What about the Catalysts?"

"Huh?" Sam asked.

"You know, because a catalyst causes action or change and—"

"I think we need an English name," James said.

"It is an . . . never mind." I thought for a second or two. "We could be Team Combustion," I suggested.

More blank looks.

"I don't know," Sam said doubtfully.

I wasn't ready to give up. "We could be—"

"The Cougars," James announced triumphantly.

The rest of the table nodded in agreement and murmured their approval.

"Great idea," I lied, wishing they'd settled on something a little more . . . clever. I started to walk away from the table.

"Wait," James called after me. "Don't you want to hang out?"

It was a kind and unexpected offer, but I was keen to get back to Chapter Four in the temporary solitude of my room.

"I'll catch up with you guys later," I said, offering the group a wave before I made my exit.

I smiled to myself as I crossed the courtyard and managed to get back to my room without seeing any sign of Owen.

Perfect!

Once I'd finished eating my delicious sandwich, I was lying on my bed, fully engrossed by life on another planet, when the door swung open.

Danny walked in, with Big Mike and T. J. right on his heels.

"Hi, Danny," I said, tucking my finger between the pages to mark my place and trying to hide my disappointment at the interruption.

"Hey," he said, crossing the room with a clenched fist.

Oh!

Was he going to punch me?

Why?

He stopped abruptly at the side of my bed and held the fist toward me.

I'm sure I looked terrified as I stared at him.

He frowned. "I'm just looking for a bump."

"A bump?"

"A fist bump," he said, looking confused. He lifted his other fist and gently tapped the two together to demonstrate.

"Is *that* what that's called?" I asked, recognizing the gesture from the NBA games I'd watched with Owen and Dad.

Danny studied me for a few seconds, before saying, "You're kind of different, aren't you, Russ?"

I'd certainly been called worse. "I suppose." I lifted my own fist for the tap and let it fall onto my chest when the greeting was complete.

"Hey, Russ," T. J. said, with a nose twitch.

Big Mike nodded at me.

"So," Danny said, "pranks."

I cleared my throat, preparing to say something that had

been on my mind since he'd mentioned it earlier. I knew it could potentially create some awkwardness, but I was compelled to express my opinion.

"Uh, I think the pranks sound . . . *fun*," I began. "But I'm just hoping no camp property will be damaged."

"No way," Danny said, shaking his head.

Whew. That was a good start.

"And no one will get hurt?" I asked.

"Geez, we're not into hurting people," Big Mike said.

"Or humiliating them?" I asked hopefully.

"Nope," Danny said. "We're talking about goofy little pranks, Russ. Just for fun."

"Great," I said, relieved.

"You should do it with us," Danny said.

"No, thanks," I said, holding up my book. "I have plans for tonight."

Danny chuckled. "Like I said before, that must be an awesome book."

"It is."

"So," T. J. said. "Are we short-sheeting beds?"

Content that no unnecessary cruelty was on their schedule, I turned my attention back to my book.

"I don't know," Big Mike said. "That's kind of a lame prank."

"That's the idea," Danny told him. "We start with something nice and simple. Then we take it up a notch every day."

"Short-sheeting today, duct taping tomorrow?" T. J. asked.

That got my attention.

"Duct taping what?" I asked, curious.

"Anything," T. J. said, with a shrug and a quick sniff. "We could tape up someone's suitcase, totally wrap their bed, or just do the doorway."

I thought about that for a second. "You'd be better off using plastic wrap in a doorway."

"What?" Danny asked. "Why?"

"The element of surprise," I explained. "If they see the duct tape, they'll stand back and admire it. But if you wrap the inside of the doorway in clear plastic—"

"They'll walk right into it," Big Mike finished for me.

Danny looked at T. J., who smiled and said, "Nice."

"I like it," Danny said. "Okay, so we'll work on that for later in the week. In the meantime, let's get started on the sheets."

"Should we just do this floor?" T. J. asked.

"Nah, let's get the whole building," Big Mike said.

"Don't forget your own beds," I said.

They all turned to stare at me.

"What?" Danny asked.

It seemed pretty obvious.

"If you play a prank on everyone but yourself, they'll know it was you."

"Oh, I didn't think of that," Big Mike said, nodding.

I propped myself up on one elbow. "And I think attempting to prank the whole building is unrealistic."

"Why?" T. J. asked, sniffing once.

"For starters, the likelihood of every room being empty is virtually nil," I explained, surprised by how much my brain was enjoying this little exercise. "Sure, some of the campers are still in the cafeteria and some are playing basketball in various places, but there's no way they're all gone."

"Good point," Danny said, nodding.

I felt a bit like Owen when I continued. "I agree that pranking both floors would be best, to help maintain your anonymity. But the question is *which* rooms and *which* beds?"

"Who is this kid?" T. J. asked, sounding rather impressed.

The three boys sat on the edge of Danny's mattress, giving me their full attention.

I made some logistical suggestions and when I was finished sharing my thoughts, Danny let out a low whistle and asked, "Are you sure you don't want to do it with us?"

"No. I just like the brainstorming part."

Big Mike gave me a look of awe. "Dude, you're a mastermind."

"Actually, I was a Master of the Mind," I told him.

"Meaning?" T. J. asked.

I took a deep breath.

Was I ready to share the tale of my complete failure as a team leader with a group of strangers?

To my surprise, I was.

And to my utter astonishment, they listened.

Defensive Rebound

Like the whole first day of camp, the first night didn't go the way I expected it to.

At all.

Instead of hanging out with the guys I'd hoped to meet and goofing off, I was alone in my room. And even worse? While I stared at the blank walls, Russ and his roommate had a party next door.

Well, maybe it wasn't a *party*, but there was a group of guys in there making a big racket. I couldn't hear what they were saying, but every now and then they all started cracking up.

And I knew for a fact that Russ wasn't funny.

He was a lot of other things (mostly brainiac-type things), but he wasn't the kind of guy who cracked people up.

Ever.

I pressed my ear against the wall, trying to figure out what was so funny, but all I heard was mumbling.

After the first few minutes, I was tempted to go knock on the door and join in. But the way Russ had been acting, I wasn't sure he'd let me. And how embarrassing would it be if my own brother shut me down in front of some of the best players at camp?

I sighed and flopped on my bed, staring at a ceiling filled with little black dots.

As I lay on the bed in that empty room, I thought about my lame performances in the first two Hoopsters sessions. I thought about eating both lunch and dinner with a kid who was more of a tagalong than a friend. And the icing on the cake was hanging out by myself while *Russ* was the life of the party.

I mean, *come on.*

I closed my eyes, wishing the day had been about a thousand times better.

I had to turn things around.

But how would I do that?

I thought for a few minutes and was amazed when I realized that making camp the most awesome week of my life would only take three steps:

Dominate on the court at every session.

Hang out with the cool kids.

Blow away an NBA player (and everyone else) at the tournament.

Wait. Make that four steps.

Win the MVP award.

Four little steps didn't sound like a big deal.

I felt my whole body start to relax, and before I knew it, I was fast asleep.

When I opened my eyes in the morning, it wasn't because I'd popped awake from excitement. No, what woke me up was the loud talking and laughing out in the hallway.

What was going on?

I glanced at my watch.

Shoot!

I only had fifteen minutes before the Hoopsters would meet for our morning run!

I rolled out of bed, wishing I'd set the stupid alarm clock.

When my feet hit the ground, I realized I'd fallen asleep totally dressed, right down to my Nikes.

I did a quick sniff test on my pits and decided I could skip the shower and roll out just the way I was.

I checked the mirror on the back of the door. Sure, I had some crazy bedhead, so my hair looked more like Russ's than my own, but that was no big deal. I pulled a sweatband (like the one the pros wore) out of the drawer and put it on.

Perfect.

But things were less perfect when I opened my door and saw all the guys heading for the stairs without me.

"Justin couldn't figure out what was wrong!" one of them said, pointing to the camper next to him. "He kept kicking his feet, trying to stretch out. It was hilarious!"

"And suspicious," the guy he'd pointed to said. "How come yours was normal?"

"Ha! You think I did it?"

"I don't know," Justin said, with a shrug.

"I'm in a double and only one of us had it," T. J. said, just as they turned the corner.

Had what?

"Me, too," someone added.

"Oh, it's on, now!" someone said, and they all laughed.

What the heck happened while I was sleeping?

What was so hilarious?

I started walking toward the stairs, wishing someone had at least knocked on my door to make sure I was up.

As I passed Russ's room, the door opened, and my brother came out, smiling.

"What are you so happy about?" I snapped.

Russ blinked a couple of times, then said, "I didn't realize happiness was forbidden."

"Very funny."

"I didn't see you at breakfast," he said.

"Yeah. I kind of slept in."

"You were up late?" Russ asked.

All the way until seven thirty. "Yeah. I was, you know, hanging out with the guys. Shooting hoops and stuff," I lied. "So, what was everybody talking about his morning? What happened?"

"Short-sheeting," Russ said, like he was an expert on it.

"Seriously?" I asked, amazed he even knew what it was. I smiled as I imagined the surprised faces, especially Big Mike's.

"I think they got about seventy percent of the building," Russ said, smiling a little wider.

"They got you?" I asked.

Russ nodded. "Danny, too."

"Oh," I said, suddenly disappointed. It was one thing for the guys in the dorm not to *hang out* with me, but how much did it stink that I wasn't even worth *pranking*?

"What's wrong?" Russ asked.

"Nothing," I told him. "I just . . . I mean, they short-sheeted my bed, too, so . . ." I didn't know what to add to the lie.

"Really?" Russ asked, surprised.

"Yeah, it was . . . *hilarious,*" I told him, forcing a smile onto my face.

I could tell his surprise had changed to something else. He looked like he felt sorry for me.

"Yes," he said quietly. "Hilarious."

"Camp is awesome, huh?"

"Uh, sure," he said, giving me a concerned look. "It's better than I expected."

Better than he expected? How was that possible, when mine was worse?

I was the one who wanted to come in the first place!

"Cool," I told him. "Hey, I've gotta get downstairs. It's time to run." I hustled to get away from him before he figured out how things were really going.

"Owen?" he called after me.

"Yeah?"

"Aren't you going to, uh . . . shower?" he asked, wrinkling up his nose.

Uh-oh. Maybe my smell test hadn't been as on target as I thought.

"Nah. It's *camp*, Russ."

"Oh," he said, frowning. "Okay, well, I'll walk down with you."

"You know what?" I said, panicked that the rest of the guys would notice my stink. "I left some stuff in the room."

"I can wait."

"No, no. Go ahead. I'll see you later."

As soon as he started to walk toward the stairs, I hurried back into my room and checked the clock.

Only *seven* minutes until the run started.

Man, I wished I'd had breakfast!

I switched out my T-shirt, shorts, and everything else as fast as I could and ran down the hallway. Halfway to the stairs, I realized I'd left the sweatband behind.

Oh well, if Russ could handle a lifetime of crazy hair, I could survive a day of it.

But the first thing I heard when I met up with the guys in front of Freeman Court was, "Nice lid," from some kid I'd never even seen before.

I didn't exactly have a comeback ready, so I ignored it.

And for most of the day, the guys ignored *me*.

I was totally wiped out after a full day of running, drills, and a pretty tough scrimmage, and when the second session of the day was over, all I wanted was my bed.

And a sandwich.

And maybe some of those cookies.

I headed over to the cafeteria and ended up pulling a total Russ. I packed a paper bag to bring back to the room and ate there by myself.

Afterward, I had a long shower, letting the hot water run over me while I tried to figure out what I was doing wrong.

Camp was a mess so far, and I had no idea how to fix it.

One of the problems was that the Hoopsters guys weren't like my friends back at Lewis and Clark. The Pioneers had known me since I was a little kid, and we were so used to each other, I never had to think about whether or not they liked me or what they thought was cool.

How was I supposed to *convince* people to hang out with me?

After my shower, I got dressed and headed for the stairs, determined to find someone to shoot hoops with.

"Hey, Owen," Jackson said, meeting up with me on the landing. "What's going on?"

Where the heck did he come from?

"Nothing," I told him, keeping my eyes peeled for someone else. Someone who could help me get more popular. Someone who was the exact opposite of Jackson.

Nice just wasn't enough.

I scanned the hallway on the first floor, but didn't see anyone.

Where was everybody?

"I heard there's ice cream in the cafeteria," Jackson said, matching my pace as I headed outside.

"I can get ice cream at home." On the weekends, anyway. When Mom was willing to buy it.

I checked the courtyard, but there was barely anyone around.

"Where are you going?" Jackson asked.

I sighed. "I don't know."

"Wanna hang out?"

It didn't look like I had a ton of options and I felt my shoulders slump as I said, "I guess."

He smiled. "What should we do?"

"We could play HORSE," I told him.

"Cool," he said, even though I could tell he'd rather go get ice cream.

I hadn't used the outdoor court yet, but it was lit up for anyone to practice on. And it was empty.

Totally empty.

What was going on?

I dribbled the ball to the free throw line. "I'll go first." After the swish, I tossed him the ball. "Your turn."

Jackson bounced it once, then threw it at the basket. It hit the backboard and fell to the concrete.

"That's *H*," I told him. "Hey, it's okay to aim first, you know."

Jackson smiled. "That's what my dad always says."

"Want a restart?"

"Nah. You go ahead."

I bent my knees a couple of times and took the shot.

Nothing but net.

This time, Jackson aimed, but his legs stayed totally stiff when he took his shot.

Air ball.

"That's O. Maybe try to loosen up a bit," I suggested.

"My dad says that, too."

"Does he practice with you much?" I was pretty sure I knew the answer. If he did, Jackson wouldn't stink.

"Sometimes. He travels most of the time, so . . ." He shrugged instead of finishing whatever he was going to say.

I walked over to the corner, slowly dribbling as I went. It was always a tricky shot for me, so I took my time and a deep breath.

Nuts!

The ball bounced off the rim and I had to chase after it. I dribbled a couple of times and bounce-passed to Jackson.

He was still working off the free throw line and he barely even touched the ball before taking a haywire shot.

Another miss.

Surprise, surprise.

I retrieved the ball and headed back to the corner. While I was getting the shot lined up, I had to ask him, "Do you *like* basketball, Jackson?"

"It's okay, I guess."

What?

I couldn't believe the kid was taking up a precious slot at Hoopsters! A kid who didn't even care was the reason Russ was stuck playing *soccer.*

Okay, the truth was that *I* was the reason Russ was stuck playing soccer.

But still.

If there'd been another open space, my brother could have filled it.

Then again, Russ seemed to be having a decent time. What was it he'd said earlier? That camp was better than he'd expected?

"I like basketball video games," Jackson suddenly said.

"What?"

"More than live basketball, I mean."

What was he talking about?

"Actually, I like all kinds of video games," he continued. "When I grow up, I'd like to design them."

"Design video games?" I asked.

"Yeah. I really like—"

He was cut off by the sound of a horde of guys racing by our court, heading for one of the big gym buildings.

"Now what?" I muttered as I watched them go. It was like the entire dorm was passing us by.

"They're going to the aquatic center," Jackson said, with a shrug.

"They?"

"You know. The Hoopsters guys."

Had I missed something on my schedule?

"Are we supposed to be there?" I asked.

"Where?"

"*The pool*," I said, getting frustrated. "Is Coach meeting everyone there?"

"What?" he asked, looking confused. "No, it's like a pool party. Just the guys."

A pool party?

Just the guys?

I was a guy!

I looked at Jackson. At least I wasn't the only one who got left out.

"I can't believe they didn't invite us," I said, shaking my head.

"Oh, I was invited," Jackson said, like it was nothing.

"What?"

"I was—"

"No, I heard you. I'm just . . . really? They invited *you*?"

"Yeah," he said, looking the way Russ did when I pointed out junk in his braces or the lameness of his high-water pants.

Like I'd hurt his feelings.

"You know what I mean," I said, slapping him on the back.

He frowned. "Not really."

"It's just . . . you're kind of . . . I mean . . . why didn't you go?"

He shrugged again. "I like hanging out with you."

"Huh," I said, thinking that over.

"We could still go, you know."

"Where, the pool?"

"Yeah. It's not like you need an invitation, Owen."

It sure seemed like it. "I didn't bring a bathing suit."

"You're wearing shorts."

He had me there.

The pool was packed with kids and when I saw how much fun everyone was having, I was glad Jackson had talked me into going.

I kind of left him behind, though, knowing it was time to meet some other people. I swam up to some guys who were playing Marco Polo and introduced myself.

"We know who you are," a guy named Chas said, and several others nodded.

I wasn't sure if he meant it in a good or a bad way. He handed me the blindfold and told me I could be "It."

I was psyched to be part of the game, so I tied it on and stood in the chest-deep water.

There was a ton of splashing and shouting coming from all over the place, so I knew it would be tough to hear the other guys.

"Marco!" I called, taking a careful step.

Somebody shouted, "Cannonball" from the deep end of the pool and there was a big splash.

"Marco!" I called again, taking another step and listening as hard as I could over all of the background noise.

I couldn't hear a single "Polo."

"You have to answer louder," I shouted. "Marco!"

Still nothing.

In fact, even the splashing had stopped.

It was . . . creepy.

I took a few more steps. "Marco!"

When there wasn't a single answer, I took off the blindfold.

I was the only one in the pool.

The guys I'd been "playing" with were all in the big Jacuzzi, laughing at me.

I couldn't believe it!

What did I ever do to them?

I climbed out of the pool and walked across the deck, ignoring the snickers and whispers I could hear from every side.

"Owen?" Jackson called out from the kiddie wading pool.

"I'll see you later," I answered, in no mood to deal with him.

For the first time I could remember, I just wanted to be alone.

Controlled Experiment

Just when I thought there might be a glimmer of hope for me and soccer, it was time for our group to move on to volleyball.

And I wasn't sure how I felt about *that*.

When we lined up in the gym, I was next to Sam and James.

"You're going to be good at this, Russ," Sam said.

I stared at him, surprised. "What makes you say that?"

He shrugged. "You're tall."

I sighed. "That isn't a free ticket to greatness."

James smiled and said, "He didn't say great; he said good."

I chuckled. "Well, I'll keep my fingers crossed."

"Except when you're serving," Sam said.

What did that mean?

"Serving what?"

"The ball," Sam said, as though it was the most obvious thing in the world.

"Wait," James said, "you've never played volleyball either?"

"Never," I told them.

"You'll be fine," Sam said, patting me on the back. "It's all about blocking."

And serving, apparently.

Coach Hernandez had been replaced with Coach Vickers, who was tall and skinny, like me. He had us stretch, warm up with jumping jacks, and run laps before giving us a brief overview of the positions and basics of volleyball.

I felt like I'd received the CliffsNotes rather than the whole story, but before I could raise my hand with the many questions racing through my mind, he was splitting us up into four teams to play.

Luckily, Sam was on my team.

"Where do I go?" I whispered as the four other players on our side of the net moved into position.

"Middle front's open," he said.

"Where's that?"

"In the middle of the front row," he said, laughing until he saw the expression on my face. "It's okay, Russ. It's just a game."

I moved to the front and awaited further instructions.

Bweep!

I winced, certain I'd be having whistle nightmares for the rest of my life.

Suddenly, a ball soared over my head. I spun around to see one of the back row players fall to his knees and hit it with his joined wrists.

"Nice one, Garrett," Sam said.

"Set!" the guy next to me shouted and tapped the ball into the air with both hands.

"Spike it, Russ!" Sam shouted.

"What?" I asked as the ball hit the floor next to me with a *thwack*.

Garrett retrieved the ball and rolled it under the net to the opposing team.

I turned to ask Sam, "Did you say *spike*?"

"Yeah," he said, then illustrated the move by jumping off the floor and swinging one arm at the air.

"I've never seen anything like that."

He squinted at me. "Do you have gym class at your school?"

"Yes," I assured him. "We played kickball in our last class before break and when I go back, we'll be doing a couple of weeks of square dancing."

"Whoa. Okay, well, this is a real sport. Like an *Olympic* sport."

I took a deep breath and waited for the ball to fly over the net again. This time, it dropped right in front of me.

"Bump it, Russ," Sam shouted.

What happened to the spiking?

I stumbled in an effort to reach the ball before it hit the floor. Amazingly, I got beneath it and sent it into the air.

"Good job!" Garrett said.

In a matter of seconds, my teammates made two hits and the ball bounced against the floor on the opposing side.

"Yes!" Sam said, slapping me on the back.

I got into position, but Garrett had moved into my space.

"Rotate," he said.

"What?"

"You gotta rotate to left front."

"But I'm playing center. I mean, middle."

Coach Vickers blew his whistle and invited me to the sideline. I attempted to high-five my replacement on the way off the court, but missed.

"This is pretty new to you, huh?" Coach said.

"I've never played before," I confessed.

To my great delight, he handed me a volleyball manual and directed me to the bench. "Assistant Coach Tanaka will go over this with you. I don't mean to pull you out, but a little tutorial will help. Just twenty minutes or so."

"Thank you!" I said, delighted by the opportunity to make some sense of the madness.

Twenty minutes was a bit optimistic on Coach's part, but for the next hour and a half, I read and studied diagrams while Coach Tanaka carefully explained what was happening on the court.

It all started to come together as I read the rules and saw how the game played out right in front of me. I liked the simple math of it. Six players on the team, three hits to send the ball over the net. And the terminology made sense, too.

Serve, bump, set, spike.

Repeat.

"Are you ready to give it a try?" Coach Vickers asked.

I glanced at the court, then back at the manual. "Would the second session be an okay time to start? I'd like to study this a bit more."

"Take your time," he said, with a smile.

✕　÷　✚

When we broke for lunch, I hurried to the cafeteria to grab some food for the room.

"Hey, Russ!" I heard Owen shout from behind me.

"Hey," I said, turning to wave.

"Come and eat with me."

"I'm heading up to my room," I told him, but the disappointed look on his face made me change my mind. I couldn't give him the cold shoulder forever.

I waited for him to fill his lunch tray and followed him to the back corner.

"There are empty tables all over the place, O."

"I like it back here."

I had the sneaking suspicion he didn't want to be seen eating with me.

Typical Owen.

When we sat down, he poked at his grilled cheese sandwich but didn't pick it up.

"Are you okay?" I asked at the exact moment he said, "Still reading that book?"

"No," I said, lifting up the volleyball manual so he could see the cover. "I'm studying."

"Volleyball."

I nodded. "Yes."

"What for?"

I stared at him. "I'm spending two full days in a gymnasium, playing this game, Owen. I'd like to have some idea of how to do it."

"Easy. Hit the ball over the net."

I smiled. "If only it were that simple. It takes a little more finesse than that. One of the most interesting—"

"I don't really want to talk about volleyball," he interrupted.

"Oh." I took a bite of my own grilled cheese. It was almost as good as Mom's. "What's going on?"

"Nothing," he said glumly.

"Owen."

He glanced at me and sighed. "Look, nothing is going the way it's supposed to."

"What does that mean?"

"I don't know. I just thought camp would be . . . different."

"Different how? You're playing basketball every day and sleeping over."

"Spending the night," he said.

"What?"

"*Sleepovers* are for seven-year-olds, Russ."

I wanted to roll my eyes, but controlled myself. "What were you expecting? Better coaches?"

"No, they're awesome."

"More drills? More playing?"

"No, it's not that at all."

"Can you give me a hint?" I asked, exasperated. Wasting time with twenty questions when I could have been cramming for volleyball was not ideal.

Finally, he told me, "It's the guys."

"What guys?"

"All of them," he said, gesturing toward the rest of the cafeteria tables.

"What about them?"

"They're"—he cleared his throat—"better than I expected."

"Well, that's good, isn't it?"

He shook his head. "I wanted to be one of the best players here. No, *the best*."

"I'm sure you are, Owen."

"I'm not," he said firmly.

"Okay, but camp isn't about being the best. It's about getting better."

He smacked his forehead in apparent frustration. "You don't get it, Russ."

I shrugged. "You're right. I don't."

"These guys don't even *talk* to me."

"On the court?" I asked, knowing how important communication was at game time.

"On it, off it, around it, and nowhere near it."

Uh-oh. It was exactly what I'd feared. He'd alienated everyone.

"Maybe you just got off on the wrong foot," I said, trying to be as kind as possible. "Give them a chance."

"They're the ones not giving *me* a chance."

I didn't know what to say. Owen was the social one of the two of us. He was the one who joked around and made friends like it was nothing. He was always surrounded by people and laughter.

"Maybe you could . . . ," I began, but didn't know where to go from there. "Maybe—"

"Never mind," he said, getting up from the table. "It doesn't matter."

Before I could say anything else, he cleared his tray into the garbage and stalked out of the cafeteria.

✖   ÷   ✚

My second session of volleyball was exponentially better than the first. This is not to say that I was an expert, or even particularly adept. It simply means that I understood the game and had a lot of fun playing it.

Later in the day, Coach lined us up and stood by the net to set the ball so we could take turns spiking.

My hits weren't the hardest and I became tangled in the net twice, but I managed to complete the move every time.

"Nice progress," Coach Vickers said, lifting his hand for a high five, which I missed.

"Thank you."

"Good job," Sam said, holding up a fist when I rejoined the line.

I made one of my own and bumped his, like I'd been doing it for years.

For the first time in weeks, I held my head high.

✖ ÷ ✚

After a delicious chicken dinner and apple pie that evening, T. J. and Big Mike came to our room for the next prank brainstorming session.

"How about the plastic-wrap doorways?" Big Mike said. "Should we do that one tonight?"

"I think it's going to take more planning," Danny said.

"What's that supposed to mean?" Big Mike asked, looking . . . *hurt.*

"We don't have enough wrap," Danny explained, looking at the rather pitiful single roll T. J. had begged from one of the cafeteria ladies.

"What about gluing the toilet lids down?" T. J. asked.

"Where will *we* go to the bathroom?" I asked him, even though my primary concern was not damaging any of the camp's property.

"Good point," he said, nodding.

For the first time that I'd seen, he didn't sniff or twitch. I smiled to myself.

He must be comfortable around me.

"We could pull a fire alarm," Big Mike suggested.

"I'm pretty sure that's against the law," Danny said.

Big Mike frowned and said, "You know, it would be cool if *someday* someone waited at least three seconds before shutting me down."

"What?" Danny asked, obviously confused.

"Never mind," he grunted. "Nobody takes me seriously."

Danny looked at me, then at T. J.

"I take you seriously," T. J. said, shrugging.

"Yeah, on the basketball court, maybe. But I'm nobody when the game's over."

"What are you talking about?" Danny asked.

He shook his head with frustration. "I'm just . . . *Big Mike.* The guy everyone wants on their team. The giant who intimidates people. Nobody gives me any credit for anything else, like having a brain."

The room was filled with stunned silence. When I realized that no one else was going to say anything, I cleared my throat.

"Well, I happen to think you were onto something with alarms."

"Whatever," Big Mike muttered.

"Not fire alarms," I said, glancing at the Hoopsters-issued stopwatch on Danny's desk. "But another kind might be a brilliant idea."

"What?" they all asked at once.

I reached for the gadget. "This is a clock, correct?"

Danny nodded. "And a stopwatch."

"Can it be set to sound intermittently?"

"Inter-what-ent-ly?" Big Mike asked, sounding just like Owen.

Owen!

"I'll be right back," I said, jumping off my bed and heading for my brother's room.

I rapped my knuckles against his door several times.

"What's going on?" he asked when he finally opened it.

"Come with me. I need your help."

"What for?" His tone was suspicious.

"Just come with me," I said, pulling his arm.

When we walked into my room together, the four boys stared at us.

"This is my brother, Owen," I said.

"No way," T. J. murmured.

"Owen, this is T. J. and Big Mike."

"We've met," Big Mike muttered, shooting Owen a dirty look.

When I glanced at the others, I saw that they were all doing the same. Even Danny.

"Listen," I told them. "You think I'm a mastermind, but that title should really go to Owen."

"Whatever," T. J. said with a *triple-twitch* of the nose.

"Whatever, yourself," Owen snapped. "I'm out of here." He started to turn toward the door.

"Wait," I said, holding his arm. "I have a plan for a prank, and I need your help."

"A prank?" Owen asked, looking interested despite himself.

And while I had everyone's attention, I laid it out for them.

When I was finished, the room was silent for a few seconds before Danny said, "I like it!"

"Okay," T. J. said, "so, we get our hands on a bunch of stopwatches and set them to go off every twenty minutes."

"Or thirty, or an hour," I said. "Whatever we decide."

"And they drive people crazy by beeping?"

"Three beeps every time it goes off," Danny said, nodding. "That would make anyone crazy."

"Wait," Big Mike interrupted. "It'll only go off once before they find it and turn it off."

"Good point," I said, causing Big Mike to smile.

"So?" Danny asked.

I glanced at Owen. "That's where he comes in."

I didn't even have to tell my brother what I needed. He was already walking around the room, inspecting every corner and piece of furniture.

"We could clip it high on the curtains," he said thoughtfully, "but that would be way too easy to find." The rest of the guys watched him peruse the bed with interest. "In between the mattress and the box spring would take a little more time."

"That's a good one," Danny murmured.

Owen looked up at the ceiling. "Hmm. Anybody got a screwdriver?"

I looked at the upturned faces and noticed something wonderful.

They were all smiling.

Blocked Pass

When we were ready to pull off the alarm prank (which was *awesome*), Russ's roommate, Danny, thought the six of us should split into pairs to get the job done quickly.

"Oh, I'm not going," Russ said.

"But it was your idea," Danny reminded him.

"I realize that, but—"

"Me, Danny, and T. J. will go together," Big Mike said, "and the *twins* can be a team." He said the word twins like he didn't believe it was true.

"No, I was—" Russ started to say, but I cut him off.

"Live a little," I told him, then looked at the rest of the group. "Let's do this!"

Russ and I headed for the lower floor, where we started knocking on doors to see which rooms were empty. If someone answered, we asked if "Chris" was there, then "realized" we were at the wrong room. If no one answered, in we went.

I couldn't believe our luck after the first three rooms. Almost all of the guys had left their stopwatches right on their desks, to be used as an alarm clock.

It was perfect.

As I hid the stopwatches in totally sneaky places, I had to admit I was impressed that Russ had come up with such a cool prank.

And I was even more impressed that he'd invited me to be in on it.

It wasn't just because I had certain skills when it came to that kind of thing. Russ knew I was lonely and he'd done something about it. Even though I was a little embarrassed to be depending on him to get me in with the cool kids, I was grateful, too.

For the next half hour or so, we kept setting timers for twenty-minute *intervals* (Russ's word) and hid them in different spots in every room. The other guys wanted to pick one spot, but I knew that once one kid figured out where the beeping was coming from, he'd tell everyone else and the prank would be over.

So, I stashed them in the toes of sneakers, the backs of closets, on top of curtain rods, and, my personal favorite, inside light fixtures.

I had a total blast!

On the way back to Russ's room, where we were all sup-posed to meet at seven o'clock, I was still thinking about the fact that none of the guys had given me the time of day before Russ invited me to join in. And now? We were hang-ing out.

I watched my brother walk ahead of me and my heart felt kind of full and swollen.

"Hey, Russ," I whispered.

"Yes?" he asked, over his shoulder.

I cleared my throat. "Thank you."

"What for?" he asked, stopping in his tracks and giving me a confused look.

I looked him straight in the eye for a few seconds, so he'd know I was serious. "Thank you."

My twin's face turned red. "No problem."

Once we were back in the room, all five of us laughed and high-fived, happy to have pulled it off.

"How many did you get?" T. J. asked.

"Eleven," I told him, hoping we'd done the most.

"No way! That's awesome."

"What was your best spot?" Big Mike asked, smiling at me for the first time *ever*.

I had to think about it for a second. "I taped one to the ductwork in a heat register. Far enough down so you can't see it in the darkness."

"Dude, you're the man!" he said, raising his hand for a fist bump.

I totally agreed.

I *was* the man.

In the morning, I was still smiling about the prank. I rolled out of bed, grabbing my towel and the bag Mom loaded with all my shampoo and junk.

I whistled all the way to the bathroom, happy that things were turning around.

I found a sink next to a tired-looking kid, brushing his teeth.

"Did they get you, too?" he asked, foamy toothpaste dribbling down his chin.

"The stopwatch?" I asked, then faked a yawn. "Yeah. It drove me crazy."

"Where was it?"

"Bottom of my suitcase. Totally buried."

"Mine was clipped to the bottom of my bed." He spit out the toothpaste. "I wish I knew who did it."

"Me, too," I said, trying to hide a smile.

After my shower, I grabbed a couple of bananas for break-fast and headed down to Freeman Court to meet the Hoop-sters for our morning run.

"Hey, Owen," Big Mike said when I got there.

T. J. and Danny both nodded at me, so I said hey and nodded back.

It was cool to have a fresh start, but before I could really talk to them, Jackson suddenly showed up next to me, out of breath and checking his watch.

He was wearing *another* Lakers jersey.

"My alarm didn't go off," he explained, through the gasps. "I mean, it went off all night, but not when I needed it to."

"Yeah." I wondered which room was his. "Mine, too."

"I barely slept," he said, yawning.

I was amazed at how well the prank had worked! "Me neither," I told him, faking a yawn of my own.

Coach blew his whistle and we started running.

Jackson kept up with me for the first few minutes, but I had my eye on the front of the pack, where T. J. and the other pranksters were in the lead. I picked up speed and left Jackson behind so I could start making my way up to them.

It was harder than I expected.

Sure, I'd been running practically every day at home, but the rest of the Hoopsters had been doing the same thing.

My breathing got pretty ragged as I passed some of the guys I didn't know, and by the time I got to Danny, I had a cramp in my side.

But I ignored it.

I ran past Danny, like it was nothing (even though it almost killed me). He glanced at me and smiled.

Then I passed him.

Take that!

Next up was Big Mike, who was surprisingly fast, considering his size.

"Hey," he said as I showed up next to him.

I didn't waste any energy on words, but nodded as I ran even faster.

See ya!

Wouldn't wanna be ya!

"This isn't a race," I heard him say.

Not officially, anyway. But if I was going to hang out with the best guys at camp, I had to show everyone that I had what it took.

T. J. was just a little ahead of me. I had to keep my pace for a minute or two, just to catch my breath. But when I came up on him, I *really* pushed it into gear.

I was a machine.

A machine built for speed.

I pumped my arms as my feet pounded the trail. The bushes on either side of me were just a blur.

I was four strides behind.

Three.

Two.

I dug deep and the next thing I knew, we were neck and neck. T. J. looked at me, all surprised, but kept his pace. I gave it another push to get past him.

"Hey!" he said when I accidentally bumped into him.

"Sorry," I called over my shoulder as I squeezed past him.

I was in the lead!

The fastest kid at Hoopsters!

That was all I needed to keep going, faster than I'd ever run before. I left the whole pack behind me on the final stretch, loving every second of it.

When I reached Coach, he clicked his stopwatch and slapped me on the back. "Nice time!"

"Thanks," I gasped, then bent over with my hands on my knees. My heart was pounding and my lungs were on fire, but I'd done it.

I'd beaten everybody!

It was seriously awesome.

T. J. stopped next to me a few seconds later. "What was that?" he demanded.

"What?"

"You pushed me."

"I didn't push," I explained. "I just bumped into you."

"You *just* knocked me off balance," he said, crossing his arms over his chest.

I peeked over my shoulder to make sure Coach wasn't listening, then back at T. J.

"Dude, what's your deal?" Big Mike demanded, standing next to T. J. and panting.

"Nothing," I told him, then turned to T. J. "Seriously, T. J., it was an accident. There was less room on the path than I thought. I'm really sorry."

And I was sorry for that.

But I wasn't sorry I'd come in first.

He looked me in the eye for a few seconds and nodded slowly. "Okay," he said. "Just don't do it again."

"I won't," I told him.

"Wow," Jackson said, running up to me, totally out of breath. "You were really moving."

"Yeah."

"I didn't know we were going for speed this morning," he said, like he was mad about it.

Didn't he get that we weren't friends?

Coach blew his whistle and we headed into Freeman Court. Me and the pranksters walked together in a tight pack, just like the Pioneers back at home.

It felt really good.

Jackson caught up with me at the ball rack.

"Hey, I heard they're serving cheeseburgers at lunch."

Did this kid think about anything besides food? I glanced at his shirt. And the Lakers?

"Cool," I told him, grabbing a ball and moving away.

Coach wanted us to split into pairs and before Jackson could catch up and ask me, I hit Big Mike up to be my partner.

"Sure," he said, following me to the far basket.

I didn't look back to see who Jackson ended up with.

I wasn't his babysitter.

"We're going to play a basketball version of Kick the Can," Coach said, once we'd all paired off. "First, decide which of you will be playing defense and who will be offense."

"Offense," Big Mike whispered.

"Okay," I said, even though that's what I would have picked.

"Now, leave the ball on the ground," Coach continued. "When I blow my whistle, one of you will be trying to reach the ball to tap it with their foot, the other will be defending it."

"Hold up," I said to Big Mike. "We're not dribbling?"

"He said to leave the ball on the floor."

"Yeah, but—"

"Just follow the instructions, Owen."

And I did. At least, I tried to.

As soon as Coach blew the whistle, Big Mike pulled a spinning move to get past me and before I could stop him, he tapped the ball with the toe of his Jordans.

What the heck?

"Good work, everybody," Coach said. "Let's do it again."

I got into a crouch, hands raised and ready. This time, when he spun, I took a couple of steps backward and tapped the ball myself.

"You're not supposed to kick it," he said. "You're supposed to stop me."

"I *did* stop you." I wasn't going to let him get past me again.

Ever.

"By cheating," he snapped.

"Cheating? Coach didn't say the defensive player couldn't kick the ball."

Big Mike looked kind of disgusted with me, but I didn't care. I was showing him (and everyone else) that I was a real player, a real Hoopster.

No more shadows and background for Owen Evans, thank you very much.

I kept him away from the ball three more times, once with a shove.

"What's your problem?" Big Mike asked, looking pretty mad.

"No problem," I told him.

"Good job, everyone," Coach said. "Now switch places."

I bent my knees and moved back and forth from one foot to the other, ready for the blast of the whistle.

"You need to relax," Big Mike said, rolling his eyes.

But he was totally wrong about that. I was in the zone.

Bweep!

I faked left, then right, then took off to the left. But Big Mike stuck to me better than I'd expected him to. By the time I got near the ball, he was standing in front of it.

I tried to get around him, but his reach was huge.

Giving up on the usual moves, I gave him an elbow to the ribs and zipped past him to tap the ball.

"Are you kidding me?" he asked.

"What?"

"This is just a drill, dude."

Sure, and on Friday it would just be a tournament . . . in front of an NBA pro.

There was no time for mercy.

By the time we split up into teams to scrimmage at the end of the session, I was on fire. I'd finally "hit my stride," as Dad would say, and I was rocking the court.

Jackson was on the opposing team and when I got the ball, I blew past him and right to the net.

Swish.

Two points for Owen Evans.

"Nice play," he called after me, kind of sarcastically.

I didn't have time for chitchat.

I went up against the best and all eyes were on me as I scored one basket after another. Somehow, I was in the right place at the right time . . . a lot.

"You know this is practice, right?" Danny asked me when I made a sweet three-pointer. "It doesn't *count.*"

"Sure," I told him.

But even if it didn't "count," it still *counted.*

Coach blew his whistle to end the session and all of us sweaty guys headed for the cafeteria.

I got in line behind T. J. and listened to him and Danny make plans to play on the outside court after they ate.

I was in, for sure!

I followed them into the eating area and we all sat at the same table, right in the center of the cafeteria, where everyone would see us. I felt like I was back at Lewis and Clark Middle School with all of my friends.

I checked around for Russ, but figured he was probably eating in his room again. I wolfed down my burger, partly because I was starving, but mostly because I couldn't wait to get out on the court with the guys.

"Owen?"

I turned to see Jackson standing at the end of the table with a tray in his hands.

"Oh, hey," I said.

"Can you scooch down a bit?"

Scooch?

"Uh, sure," I said, starting to move down the bench. Then I saw that the rest of the guys were finished with their lunches and starting to get up. "Oh, you can have my spot. I'm heading out."

I shoved the last bite of burger into my mouth and washed it down with a gulp of milk.

"Heading out?" he asked, looking confused.

"The guys invited me to shoot hoops." Not *officially* or anything, but they knew I was listening when they were talking about it and that was pretty much the same thing.

I waited for Jackson to nod like he understood, but he just stared at me.

"So, I'm going to go," I told him, pointing at the exit with my thumb.

"Now?"

"Yeah. Now."

He put his tray on the empty table. "What's the deal, Owen?"

I glanced over my shoulder and saw T. J. walking out the door.

"The deal is, the guys are waiting for me," I said.

"So, you don't have two seconds to talk to me?"

"Maybe later, okay?" Before he could answer, I grabbed my tray and dropped it off in the dish area.

Jackson had slowed me down so much I had to sprint to catch up with my new friends.

Complementary Angles

My second day of volleyball might not have been considered a triumph by some people, but I was very happy with it.

It was amazing what a little bit of studying had done for my game, and I wished someone (like Owen) had directed me to a basketball manual or two when I'd joined the Pioneers. I had no doubt it would have made things a lot easier.

It turned out that I liked the mechanics of volleyball, from the clocklike rotation of players, to the back and forth turns at serving. It felt very logical to me, and I'd always been a big fan of logic.

As it turned out, my height *did* help when it came to blocking, but the move I liked the most in the sport was setting the ball.

There was an element of geometry involved when it

came to directing it into the perfect position for a spike. I thoroughly enjoyed calculating the angles required for the spiking player to hit a target on the opposing team's side, not to mention anticipating the ball's trajectory.

It was fascinating.

I'd fully expected that volleyball and I would part as enemies when the two days were up, but when we finished our final session, I was sad to see it end.

"Want to head to the caf?" Sam asked when Coach released us.

"Absolutely. I'm starving."

I was even hungrier when I saw stir fry on the menu.

Once I'd filled my plate with a mixture of noodles, vegetables, and chicken, I found Sam and several of the Cougars sharing a table.

I couldn't help scanning the dining area for signs of my brother. When I didn't see him, I assumed he'd succeeded in making some Hoopster friends and was busy with them.

Mission accomplished.

"Mind if I sit here?" someone asked.

I turned to see Owen's friend Jackson standing next to our table.

"Not at all," I assured him, moving down the bench to make room.

Jackson settled in next to me and I introduced him to Sam and the rest of my team.

"No Owen?" I asked as I took a bite of broccoli.

Jackson shook his head. "He's been pretty busy."

And Jackson wasn't? "But you're in the same camp."

He swallowed a mouthful. "I mean he's been busy with some of the other guys."

"The other Hoopsters?" I asked.

"Yeah. Big Mike, Danny . . ."

"I see," I said, picturing the situation all too easily.

Abandoning a friend like Jackson in favor of "cooler" people was the kind of behavior I should have expected from Owen. He'd made leaps and bounds in terms of being a better person this year, but it was far too easy for him to backslide into Jerkdom.

Sometimes I wondered if he'd ever truly grow up.

"So, how do you like camp so far?" Jackson asked the group.

"I love it," Sam told him. "I'm learning a ton of stuff."

"And there are some awesome guys here," James added.

Jackson looked to me and I told him, "It's going better than I'd expected."

He studied me for a moment. "What were you expecting?"

"To have a terrible time," I admitted.

"Really?" Sam asked.

James looked curious. "Why did you sign up?"

"Well, the truth is, I was kind of forced . . . no, *convinced* to come."

Jackson looked surprised. "Me, too."

"By who?"

"My dad," he said. "What about you?"

Even though Owen had treated him unkindly, I didn't want Jackson to know what a creep my brother could be, so I glossed over the events that had brought me to camp.

"My dad wanted me to come," Jackson explained when I was finished, "because he knows some of the coaches and stuff." He paused. "I'm not exactly the best player."

I told him the same thing I'd said to Owen. "Camp is about getting better, not being the best."

"Could you tell my dad that?" Jackson asked, half smiling. "The truth is, I'd rather be at computer camp."

"Learning what?" I asked.

"Video game design."

"Cool," James said. "That would be awesome."

"That's what I'd like to do when I'm older. Be a designer."

"Your dad doesn't like that idea?" I asked.

Jackson laughed. "I haven't been able to tell him. It's kind of . . . complicated."

"Are you having a decent time here, anyway?" Sam asked him.

"Yeah. I mean, it's better than the last couple of camps I went to. Owen's fun to hang out with. I mean, he *was*."

The longer we sat and chatted, the more ashamed I was of my brother. Jackson was a really nice kid and all he'd wanted was a friend at camp.

It was too bad he'd chosen Owen.

We'd almost finished eating when it caught my attention

that almost every boy who walked by our table either said hi to Jackson or gave him a high five.

I glanced at Sam, who appeared to have noticed, too.

"How do you know all of these people?" Sam asked, apparently as intrigued as I was when yet another group passed by with nods, smiles, and greetings for Jackson.

He smiled faintly. "I don't," he said. "I mean, I know a couple of them, but not everyone. Like I said before, it's complicated."

Sam looked at me with a raised eyebrow, then asked Jackson, "So, what's the story?"

When our new friend explained, it all made perfect sense.

$$\times \quad \div \quad +$$

That night, the guys and I were brainstorming in my room and I was thinking about how glad I was that Danny had forgotten about stacking our beds. I liked the room just the way it was.

There was a knock on the door.

I knew exactly who it was, and felt tempted not to answer it.

But he was my brother.

"Owen," I said, by way of explanation as I got to my feet.

"Great," T. J. muttered.

When I saw the expressions on the rest of the faces, I knew they were equally unenthusiastic.

Hmm.

I thought they'd become friends.

I swung open the door and was surprised to see not Owen, but Jackson standing there.

"Oh," he said, seeing the crowd behind me. "I didn't know you were busy."

"We aren't," Danny called to him. "Come on in."

"I can come back," he said quietly to me.

"It's fine," I told him, moving to the side so he could enter the room.

T. J. made space for him on the bed, Big Mike handed him a bottle of water and a couple of cafeteria cookies, and then all of the guys silently smiled at him.

Jackson looked as uncomfortable as I felt. And, thanks to our lunchtime conversation, I knew exactly why.

He cleared his throat. "So, I was just wondering if anyone wanted to maybe shoot some hoops or something."

"Definitely," Danny said, jumping off the bed.

"For sure," T. J. exclaimed, pulling on his hoodie.

"Uh, guys?" I said. "What about our . . . plans?"

Danny looked at the others, then said, "I think we should skip a night."

"Really?" I asked, surprised.

"Good idea," Big Mike agreed. "That will throw everybody off."

I had to admit, he had a point. Leaving everyone to anticipate a prank that wouldn't happen was kind of a prank in itself.

Clever!

All of the guys were standing and Danny had pulled a basketball from the bottom of our closet. The group started toward the door.

"Aren't you coming, Russ?" Jackson asked.

"To play basketball? Uh, no. I thought I would—"

"Read?" T. J. and Danny said at the same time.

"Well, yes," I said, glancing at the track-and-field manual I'd borrowed in advance. I was going to go into the next round of sports somewhat prepared.

The guys filed into the hallway, but Jackson lingered behind.

"You're really not coming?" he asked quietly.

"They're good guys," I told him. "I know they're kind of acting like everyone else right now, but that will wear off once you get out there."

"I don't know," he said reluctantly.

"Just give them a chance, Jackson. I'm glad that I did."

He thought about it for a moment, then slowly nodded. "Okay. I'll see you later."

Once I was alone in the room, I flipped my borrowed book open to the chapter on pole vaulting.

The diagrams looked more than a little intimidating, and my whole body stiffened at the thought of being hurled into the air. But as I read, my shoulders started to relax as I recognized a very comforting fact. Just like volleyball and, now that I thought about it, probably every sport on earth, there was an element of science behind it.

In this case, it was physics.

And I loved physics.

Pretty soon, I had a notepad out and was making calculations based on the speed I could (hopefully) run down the track, the angle my body needed to achieve, and the amount of bending the pole would require to push me into the air while snapping back into a straight position.

It all boiled down to velocity, energy (both potential and kinetic), and angles.

I smiled to myself. On paper, it was simple.

There was a knock on the door.

"Who is it?" I called, unwilling to leave the desk.

"Who do you think?" Owen asked.

Great.

"Come in."

"Hey," he said, crossing the carpet and flopping on my bed. "Where is everybody? I thought we'd be getting ready for the next prank."

I glanced at him. "There is no next prank."

"What?"

"The guys figured that keeping everyone on their toes in preparation for *nothing* would be a good prank," I explained. "Kind of brilliant, really."

His shoulders slumped. "That stinks."

"So, I'm taking the time to—"

"Read," he finished for me.

I was going to say "prepare for the challenge of track and field," but he didn't care.

"So, where'd they go?" he asked.

"Who?"

"Duh, Russ. Danny and those guys."

"They left a while ago to play basketball with Jackson."

"Shooting hoops?" he said, then his eyes bulged. "Wait, with Jackson?"

"That's what I said."

"But . . . why?"

"This is Hoopsters camp, Owen. They wanted some—"

"I mean, why did they go with *Jackson*?"

Wait.

Was it possible that Owen didn't know?

No.

Everyone knew.

But if he knew, wouldn't Owen be acting the same way as everybody else?

"Why do you think?" I asked, genuinely curious.

He shrugged. "They were probably short a guy. But don't they know *my* room is right next door?" He paused to think about it. "Maybe they knocked while I was in the shower or something."

"Maybe."

"Are they playing on the outdoor court?" he asked.

"I have no idea."

"*Hmm.* I should probably head down there and sub in. Jackson isn't exactly a star player."

I decided to test the water. "But people seem to like him." Even if they didn't really know him. "I thought you did, too."

"He's okay, I guess. But he's been kind of glued to me since we got here. I finally cut him loose today, since it was cramping my style."

Unbelievable.

"I wasn't aware that being an egomaniac was a style."

"Huh?" he asked distractedly as he pushed aside the curtain to search for the glow of "star" players.

"Never mind."

"Okay," he said, letting the curtain drop back into place. "I'm heading out there to save them from lameness."

I sighed, amazed at his arrogance. I wasn't going to be the one to tell him about Jackson.

"See you later," I said as he left the room.

In the morning, I met up with Sam and James outside the cafeteria. We each had scrambled eggs, toast, and a couple of pieces of bacon.

"Are you ready for this?" Sam asked.

"Track and field? I hope so."

"You'll probably be good at hurdling and the long jump,

since you're tall," James said, piling some eggs onto his toast and shoving it into his mouth.

"Why does everyone *still* think tall is the answer?" I asked.

James shrugged. "You need long legs for some of this stuff. My brother's over six feet tall and he's awesome at . . . well, *everything*."

"Mine, too," Sam said.

"It stinks, doesn't it?" James asked.

"Totally. I'm never going to be as good as my brother at sports."

"Me neither," James said, shaking his head. "Mine will probably get a college scholarship for baseball."

"Mine's been scouted for football since he was fifteen."

"No way."

"Seriously," Sam said. "I'm doomed."

"We both are," James said, starting to smile.

The two of them shrugged, as though their fates were sealed, then started laughing.

I chuckled as I kept my eye out for my own brother.

When Danny had arrived back in the room the night before, I'd asked whether Owen had joined their game and he'd simply stated, "We had enough guys."

I'd felt the usual urge to feel sorry for Owen, but it was overridden by the feeling that he'd gotten exactly what he deserved. If he treated people like Jackson poorly, he should expect to receive the same kind of treatment himself.

I spotted him with a tray of food and studied him for a moment.

He was scanning the room and I knew that he wasn't looking for an empty seat, but someone "cool" to sit with. He started to look frustrated, then desperate.

Our eyes met and he smiled as he started to walk toward us.

I don't think so, dear brother.

"Ready?" I asked Sam and James as I shoved the last piece of toast into my mouth and practically choked on it.

"Are you okay?" Sam asked, handing me a glass of water.

I washed the dry bread down my throat with relief. "Thank you," I told him. "I'm fine. Are you ready to go?"

He looked puzzled, then pointed at the remaining food on his plate. "I was just going to—"

Owen was getting closer.

"We should probably get to the gym a bit early, don't you think?" I asked James.

"Oh, uh . . . sure," he said, picking up his own remaining toast with one hand and his tray with the other.

The teammates followed me toward the aisle.

"Russ!" Owen exclaimed as he arrived at our table.

"Hey, O," I said. "You can have this spot. We're just leaving."

"What?" he asked, then frowned. "The session doesn't even start for fifteen minutes. I thought we could—"

"We've got to go," I said, with an apologetic shrug. "Right, Sam?"

"Right," he said, following behind me.

Once we were out of earshot, James asked, "What was that about?"

"Sometimes my brother needs a little time to himself."

MVP

Russ was giving me the cold shoulder and I had no idea why.

I knew for a fact that I hadn't done anything to him. Yes, I'd put some pressure on him to come to camp, but he'd had a better time than he expected to.

He should have been thanking me.

I tried to talk to him in his room, in the cafeteria, and even in the courtyard on Wednesday morning, but he brushed me off every time.

Danny and the Hoopsters guys seemed to be busy whenever I ran into them. Half the time, Jackson was with them, which made zero sense. I was a thousand times better at basketball than he was and I couldn't understand why they wanted to shoot hoops with a kid who wasn't very good.

When Jackson wasn't with the pranksters, he still hung

out with me. I had to admit, it was kind of nice to have someone to talk to in the cafeteria and stuff, but I couldn't help wishing that the someone was . . . cooler.

"Did you try the coleslaw?" Jackson asked when we were having lunch in the cafeteria on Wednesday. "It's awesome!"

I stared at him, wondering how it was possible for a kid to be more fired up about coleslaw than basketball.

"It's okay," I told him.

"Hey, Jackson," one of the guys I didn't know said, giving him a high five on the way by.

I bit into my hot dog, wishing I'd gone a little heavier on the ketchup.

"So, you wanna hit the pool tonight?" Jackson asked.

"Who's going?"

He shrugged. "Us, if you want to."

Just the two of us? *Boring.*

"What are Danny and those guys doing?"

"I don't know." He swallowed a mouthful of slaw. "We don't have to swim. We could do something else."

I figured that my brother and the rest of the guys would be planning a prank for that night, and I wanted to be part of it.

"I kind of have some stuff to do," I told him.

I was frustrated with the kid. I wanted to have an awesome time at camp, and that meant hanging out with other guys, not just babysitting Jackson.

"What's going on, Owen?" he suddenly asked.

"What?"

"We used to hang out and now—"

"*Used to hang out?* We've only known each other for a few days."

"You know what I mean. I thought we were friends."

"Hey, man," another camper said.

Jackson nodded back and bit into his hot dog.

"Sure, we're friends," I said. "Or you know, whatever."

He frowned. "Well, are we or aren't we?"

"What? Friends?"

"It's a pretty simple question, Owen."

"Sure. I guess."

He squinted at me, like he was realizing something. "When it's convenient."

"Huh?"

"You're my friend when there's no one else around."

I looked from one end of the cafeteria to the other. "There's gotta be two hundred guys in here and I'm sitting with you."

He blinked hard. "Wow. Am I supposed to thank you or something?"

"No, I—"

"Are you doing me a favor by sitting here?"

"What?"

He waved his hand, like he was dismissing me. "Just go."

What was his problem?

"Fine," I said, standing up.

I carried my tray over to the garbage and when I looked back at Jackson's table, four more Hoopsters had sat down with their lunches.

Good. They could keep him busy for a while.

That night, I dropped by Russ's room, hoping Danny and the gang would be there. But they weren't. And Russ was nose-deep in a book, as usual.

The room was totally quiet, except for the sound of pages turning, and it was driving me nuts.

I wanted Russ to say something, *anything*, but it didn't happen.

I was looking out the window and spotted Jackson crossing the courtyard on his way to the cafeteria for dinner. He was wearing *another* Lakers jersey with Farina's name and number on the back.

Come to think of it, every Lakers shirt I'd seen him wear had Farina's name on it.

"I'm surprised he even has a favorite *team*, let alone a favorite *player*," I muttered.

"Uh-huh," Russ mumbled, not even looking up from the book.

I knew he wasn't listening, but I kept talking, anyway.

"As far as I can tell, the guy has about six thousand Farina jerseys and he doesn't even like basketball."

"Who?" Russ asked, suddenly interested.

"Jackson."

He fixed his glasses. "What about him?"

"Are you in or out of this conversation, Russ?"

He squinted at me. "That depends on what you're going to say."

"I'm just surprised he'd wear Farina gear in Oregon."

Russ frowned. "Wouldn't you?"

I laughed. "Okay, first of all, I'm not a Lakers fan. Duh, Russ."

"But he's—"

"And if I was, I'd be all about Kobe."

"Instead of Farina," Russ said, like he was making sure he'd heard me right.

Since when was *he* into Farina?

"Yeah."

"Even if he was your dad?"

"What?" I blinked hard, totally confused. "If who was my dad?"

"Farina," Russ snapped.

What the heck?

"Okay, I don't even know what you're talking about."

Russ sighed, like I was the one who wasn't making any sense. "What is Jackson's last name?"

I rolled my eyes. "Duh. It's Jackson."

Russ held his head in his hands. "No. It's Farina. Roberto Farina is his *father*, Owen."

I gulped. "Roberto Farina from the Lakers?"

"What do you think? The perfectly nice kid you ditched is *Jackson Farina*."

"No way," I gasped. "Why didn't he tell me? Why didn't *anyone* tell me?"

Russ shrugged. "They probably assumed you already knew."

"But I didn't!"

"You've made that abundantly clear."

"He can't be. He's not even a good player."

"Basketball skills aren't genetic, Owen."

"*Everyone* knows who he is?" I asked, still in shock.

Russ rolled his eyes. "You haven't noticed how the guys treat him?"

"What?"

"The smiles, the nods, the high fives, the—"

"Wait a second," I said as a bunch of images flashed in my head. Russ was right. Guys were always saying hi, waving at him, and during lunch that very day, Jackson's table had filled up the second I walked away.

Whoa!

Had they been waiting for me to leave?

"So, you *have* noticed," Russ said, interrupting my thoughts.

"I guess so. But I wasn't really paying attention."

He shook his head. "Surprise, surprise."

I thought back to the things Jackson had said about his

dad. There were basketball tips, but he'd also mentioned his dad knew some of the coaches at camp.

Oh.

Oh no.

My head was spinning. "Hold on. Does that mean we'll be playing in front of *Roberto Farina* on Friday? Is he our special guest?"

Russ shrugged. "I have no idea what special guest you're referring to, but Jackson told me his father would be here at the end of camp."

"I can't believe this." I groaned.

"What?"

"That I ditched the wrong guy."

Russ made one of those faces at me that I hated. It was the you're-a-total-jerk face.

"Are there *right* guys to ditch?"

Oh, brother. "Not now, Russ." The last thing I needed was a lecture from Nerdenstein.

"What? Why did you do it, anyway? Jackson seems like a really nice guy."

"Yeah, yeah," I said, distracted. "He's nice."

Farina would be presenting the MVP award?

"And that's not enough?"

I sighed. "It's Hoopsters, Russ."

"I'm aware of that. Why wasn't a nice friend enough?"

"Because I wanted to hang out with some *Hoopsters*-type guys."

Russ stared at me, like he couldn't believe we were related. I knew that look, too. I used it on him all the time.

"Well, I guess this is an example of why you can't judge a book by its cover."

"Yes, you can," I snapped, then pointed to the one he was holding. The cover had a bunch of triangles and circles and junk on it. He was always reading that stupid sci-fi stuff. "I'll bet that one's full of boring fake space stuff."

Russ raised one eyebrow at me. "Interesting."

"No, it's not. That's my whole point."

My brother flipped the book over and read the cover out loud to me. "*Basic Principles of Track and Field.*" He looked up at me. "Point made."

"Whatever." It was time to change the subject. "So, where's Danny?"

Russ shrugged. "Doing *Hoopsters-type guy stuff,* I guess."

"Very funny."

"I'm guessing you weren't invited."

"No," I admitted.

"So, now you know how Jackson feels."

I was about to argue the point, until I realized that Russ was right. Me and Jackson had both been left out.

He'd tagged along after me, just like I'd tagged along after the Hoopsters.

That was super embarrassing.

I sat on Danny's bed. "So, how am I supposed to fix this?"

"That depends. Which part do you want to fix?"

"All of it," I told him. "Well, mostly the Jackson part."

"Because his dad is a Laker?"

"No. Well, yes, but mostly because . . ." I thought about how it felt to be left behind by Danny and the guys, I thought about that rotten night in the pool where I played Marco Polo by myself, all that time alone in my room while everyone else was having fun. I thought about how it felt not to know *why* I was left out, or to know how to change it.

"Owen?" Russ said, snapping me out of it.

"Because they made me feel crummy." I blinked. "I mean, because *I* made *him* feel crummy." I cringed when I said it, knowing it was true. I'd made Jackson feel as bad as the other guys had made me feel.

And that stunk.

Russ waited a minute before saying anything. "So, talk to him."

"And say what?"

"That you're sorry," Russ said, like it was the easiest and most obvious thing in the world.

On the way to apologize, I realized I didn't even know the kid's room number. I'd been hanging out with him all week, and I had no idea where he lived.

I asked around, and when I tracked down his room, I knocked on the door, nervously trying to think of what to say.

"Oh," Jackson said, frowning. "I thought you had *stuff to do* tonight."

On top of everything else, I was a liar.

Sure, I'd *hoped* to have plans, but the pranksters had left me in the dust.

Just like I'd left Jackson.

"No. I mean, yeah . . . but I wanted to talk to you."

"To me?" He made a mock bow. "What an honor."

"Jackson. I'm serious."

He glared at me. "About what?"

"Wanting to talk. Just give me a minute, okay?"

"Fine," he said, opening the door wider so I could walk inside. "This should be good."

The first thing I saw was a picture of Jackson and his dad, sitting right on his desk. If I'd paid him one stinkin' visit, I would have *known*.

"So," I said, but didn't know where to go from there.

"So," he echoed, sitting on the edge of his desk.

"I wanted to tell you I'm sorry," I blurted, nice and fast, like ripping off a Band-Aid.

"For what?" he asked, crossing his arms.

For a lot of things. "For the way I've been acting. You know, taking off on you and stuff."

"You're busy," he said, rolling his eyes. "Right?"

"Yeah, but . . . well, not *that* busy."

He didn't say anything, so I figured I should try a different angle.

"Why have you been hanging out with me, Jackson?" I asked. "I haven't been very . . . nice."

He shrugged. "At first, that's what I liked about you."

"What?" I choked.

He sighed. "Do you know what it's like to be related to an NBA player?"

I wished!

"Uh, no."

"It stinks. People try to buddy up with you, just so they can meet him. You never know who your real friends are."

"I guess that *would* kind of stink."

"Kind of? I'm not just talking about Hoopsters, Owen. It's at school and everywhere else, too." He glanced at me. "You were different. You didn't act super nice just because of who my dad is."

I took a deep breath. "I didn't know."

He looked surprised. "Didn't know what?"

"That he's your dad."

Jackson frowned. "You didn't? But our last name is on almost everything I wear."

I shrugged. "I thought he was your favorite player."

He shook his head, like he couldn't believe what he was hearing. "It's seriously my whole wardrobe, Owen. I mean, I have Farina *socks*."

"And I have Blazers T-shirts, sweatshirts, shorts, and hats," I said. "If they sold Blazers underwear, I'd buy some."

I was relieved when he cracked a smile.

He nodded slowly. "Okay, so you thought I was just a Farina fan. No, make that his *biggest* fan." He was quiet for a moment. "Which means you weren't hanging out with me because I'm his kid."

"Not at all."

But I would have, if I'd known.

"So, why did you blow me off?"

"I don't know," I said, shaking my head. "I had this idea about Hoopsters-type guys and how cool it would be to hang out with the elite players and stuff."

"Why aren't you with them now?"

I sighed. "They don't want to be around me, Jackson. Like you, they figured out that I'm a . . . jerk."

"Yeah, well, they wouldn't have to be detectives for that."

He was right. I'd left a ton of clues.

I took a deep breath. "Look, you were the only kid here who wanted anything to do with me. I could have had fun with you and made a good friend, but I ditched you for the cooler guys."

That didn't come out right.

"The cooler guys." He half smiled and looked away. "Wow. You really *are* a jerk." He paused. "A total jerk."

"I know."

The room was totally silent until he said, "But you're

here now, admitting you were wrong." He glanced back at me. "You *are* admitting you were wrong, right?"

"Yes. Totally."

"Hmm. So, maybe you're *slightly* less of a jerk than you were a couple of minutes ago."

"Thanks a lot."

"Hey, it's an improvement." He paused. "Do you really feel bad about blowing me off? Honestly?"

"Yeah." It was the truth.

He was quiet for a moment. "Do you *want* to be friends with me, Owen?"

What I'd said before was totally true. He was the only kid at camp who'd wanted anything to do with me, and I'd treated him like he wasn't worth my time.

I nodded. "Yeah, I do."

"Because my dad's Roberto Farina?"

"Roberto who?" I asked, trying to make a joke. "Oh, you mean the NBA superstar. No, I want to be friends with you because you're . . . you know. *You.*"

He lifted a fist for me to bump. "Cool."

"That's it?" I couldn't believe he was letting me off that easily. "Wait, why are you giving me another chance?"

"My dad," he said, with a shrug.

"What?"

"He always says that if you can forgive someone, you should."

How lucky was that? I'd been expecting a whole lot

worse from Jackson, but telling him I was sorry (and really meaning it) was enough.

Sweet!

Jackson cleared his throat. "Owen?"

"Yeah?"

"I can only forgive you once."

I looked him right in the eye, so he'd know I understood. "That's all I need."

Chain Reaction

We'd spent most of Wednesday running. And when I say running, I don't mean laps. *We sprinted.*

It turned out that aside from physics, the common element that would be shared by our track activities was speed.

And I didn't have any.

After a full day of working on starting, running, and finishing, I knew that day two was going to be rough.

So, when I woke up on Thursday morning, I had to drag my aching body to the gym for another round.

"Okay, guys," Coach Bennett said. "Yesterday, we learned the fundamentals of speed. Today, we're going to use it."

Everyone around me sounded excited and I followed the group over to the row of aluminum hurdles Coach had placed on the track.

I'd studied the diagrams in my book, so I knew what my body was supposed to do. I just wasn't sure that it *could*. In addition to speed, hurdling would require timing and coordination. And on that particular morning, I doubted I had *any* of those things.

Coach Bennett went over the basics with us and when he blew his whistle, we lined up to jump over one.

Just one.

I took a deep breath from my place at the back of the line.

"Are you okay?" Sam asked.

"Sure," I told him, watching as the first of our teammates charged at the hurdle. I watched his feet and when he got close, I counted off Coach's recommended four steps before the jump.

He led with his right foot and soared over the obstacle like it was nothing and the whole lineup cheered.

When the next runner was up, he did the exact same thing and cleared the hurdle. The third bumped it with the tip of his shoe, but it merely wobbled for a second, then became still again.

"Nice," Sam said.

"Hey, my brother could jump a hurdle twice that size," James joked.

"Oh yeah? Mine could do it backward," Sam countered, and they both laughed.

"Just do your best," James said.

And Sam did. When it was his turn, he took off at the blast of Coach's whistle and made a perfect leap.

"Next," Coach said.

I nodded as I stepped up to the line. I took a deep breath, then another.

You're tall.

You have long legs.

You can do this.

I inhaled deeply again and exhaled slowly.

"Ready?" Coach asked.

I nodded and when he blew his whistle, I took off as quickly as I could.

One, two, three . . . no, don't count yet!

The closer I got to the hurdle, the taller it was.

I took a few more steps.

Count now! Four more!

Wait, is it too late?

At the very last second, instead of jumping, I veered sharply to my right and ran around the hurdle. I stumbled slightly, but stayed upright.

"Okay," Coach said. "That was a good dry run. Let's give it another try."

Embarrassed to be the only one who had faltered, I returned to the starting line with hot and undoubtedly bright red cheeks.

"You can do it," James said, patting me on the back.

Considering how nice the Cougars had been all week, I shouldn't have been surprised by the "you had good speed" and "just go for it" that followed from the other guys.

I nodded and took another deep breath as I stepped on the starting line.

"Let's go, Russ," Sam encouraged from behind me.

Coach Bennett blew his whistle and I took off again, feeling every step in my aching muscles.

I heard some cheering behind me, and when the moment came, I counted off the steps.

One, two, three.

On four, I leaped, extending my right leg as far ahead of me as it could go and lifting my body off the ground.

I was flying through the air, amazed that I could do it.

And then, suddenly, I wasn't doing it at all.

My left shoe caught the hurdle, right on my laces, and I didn't have time to shake free. The next thing I knew, I was heading face-first onto the track.

Uh-oh.

I threw my hands out in front of me and landed hard, then somersaulted a couple of times before coming to a stop.

I waited to hear laughter from the starting line.

But there was none.

Instead, I heard the pounding of footsteps as my teammates and Coach ran over to make sure I was okay.

To my utter amazement, I was.

Sure, I felt embarrassed, and my palms were a bit scraped, but I was fine.

The fall hadn't killed me.

"You were so close," Sam said.

"You missed it by a couple of inches," James added, demonstrating with his fingers how far I'd been from clearing the obstacle.

"Would you like to sit out for a few minutes?" Coach asked, once he'd helped me to my feet.

I looked at the faces of my teammates, who were obviously eager for me to succeed at something I'd never even imagined trying.

And that made me want to succeed, too.

"Can I give it another try?" I asked Coach.

"Attaboy," he said, with a smile.

As is often the case with new things, the third time was a charm. I knew what it felt like to avoid the obstacle and I knew what it felt like to crash into it. Somehow, that gave me the confidence to give it all I had.

It probably wasn't the most graceful hurdle the world had ever seen. I'm sure my arms were flailing and I can only imagine the crazed expressions on my face as I took off, cleared it, and landed safely on the other side.

I wasn't a natural, but I did it.

My teammates cheered.

Coach patted me on the back and said, "Nice work, kid."

The rest of the morning went just as well. I had some rocky moments when we added more hurdles and timing became an even bigger issue. But I did my best, just like everyone else.

When we broke for lunch, I walked over to the cafeteria with the rest of the Cougars. We talked and laughed as we filled our plates with pasta, garlic bread, and salad.

Sam found a table that had room for all of us and we sat down to enjoy the meal.

I was barely two bites in when I felt a tap on my shoulder.

"Hey, Russ," Owen said when I turned around.

"Hey."

"Can I talk to you?"

"Sure," I said, making room next to me. "What's going on?"

"I patched things up with Jackson," he said. "I came by your room to tell you last night, but—"

"I was asleep by eight th—"

"You didn't answer," he interrupted, before I could tell him about my exhausting first day of track and field.

"I'm glad you worked it out," I told him. "I like Jackson."

"Me, too. But the thing is, I can't figure out how to deal with the other guys."

"Talk to them, Owen. They're just people."

He shook his head. "They won't listen."

"Then try again."

"You don't get it, Russ. Jackson told me they think I'm a ball hog—"

"Which you have been, right?"

"Yeah, I guess so. But they also think I'm too aggressive—"

"Accurate?" I asked.

"Um . . . maybe. Jackson wouldn't tell me which guy said it, but one of them thinks I'm a showboat."

I stared at him. "Would you agree?"

He groaned. "You're not helping, Russ."

"Well, would you?" I pushed.

"I guess, but I just wanted to show them what I could do," he said, shoulders slumped.

I thought about it for a minute before I told him, "Then maybe that's the solution."

"What?"

I adjusted my glasses. "Maybe I was wrong—"

He laughed. "Wow, could I have that in writing?"

"I said *maybe*, Owen." I gave him a long look and waited for the smile to leave his face. "Can I continue?"

"Yeah."

"*Maybe* I was wrong to suggest talking to them, when the fact is, your actions speak the loudest."

"Is this some kind of a riddle?"

I sighed. "No. What I'm saying is that you need to *show* these guys that you aren't a ball hog by passing to them. Be less aggressive. Don't be a showboat."

"But—"

"*Show them* you're a good player and a good teammate. I

know for a fact that you're already both of those things for the Pioneers."

"I know, but it's Hoopsters camp and—"

"You don't have to turn into someone else, Owen. Who you are is enough."

He thought about that for a moment or two, then smiled at me. "Thanks, Russ."

"You're welcome," I said, starting to turn my attention back to my pasta.

"You know something?" Owen asked. Before I had a chance to respond, he continued, "I can see why your Masters of the Mind team made you their leader."

My fork stopped halfway to my mouth and I was going to ask him what he meant.

But he was gone.

$$\times \quad \div \quad +$$

During the afternoon session of track and field, I let Owen's words simmer in my mind. Of course, I also concentrated on what Coach was saying, but my brother's comments gave me a warm, satisfied feeling at the same time.

We moved on from hurdles to long jump, which proved to be wonderfully easy in comparison. To my surprise, I ranked third on the team for longest jump.

Pole vaulting was a slightly different story, but once I'd

taken a couple of practice runs and reminded myself it was simply a matter of physics, I managed to heave myself over the bar.

My landing was atrocious, but the thick mattress that caught me certainly helped.

As I walked back to the line, I felt taller than usual. It took me a moment to realize that I'd abandoned the slouched shoulders that had weighed me down since the mess at state.

Hmm.

It seemed that despite the fact that none of the sports and activities I'd been involved with all week had anything to do with Masters of the Mind, they'd helped me find my way back.

The pranks had brought me back to brainstorming.

I'd found physics and geometry in the most unlikely places.

I'd made friends and shown them that I wasn't the sort of person who gave up.

And that's when it hit me.

There was no reason to give up on Masters of the Mind.

We'd suffered a setback at state. A bump in the road. A blip on the radar.

An aluminum hurdle in the middle of a sprint.

Next time, we would jump over it.

It was as simple as that.

I found myself smiling as I stepped into my place at the back of the line.

"Why are you so happy?" James asked when I joined him.

I grinned at him, but didn't answer.

There were too many reasons to list.

In the Paint

I knew my brother was smart, but it always surprised me when he wasn't just textbook, classroom, nerd herd smart, but *people* smart.

When I left him in the cafeteria, I headed down to the chip trail to walk and think for the rest of my lunch hour.

Russ was right about being myself.

There was a reason I hadn't made a bunch of friends at camp like I had at home. I thought back to the night in the pool, when I was the only guy playing Marco Polo. My Pioneer teammates would have done the exact same thing if someone had acted the way I did.

No one wants to hang around with a jerk.

As I walked, I wished I hadn't wasted so much of the week trying to wow everybody and be a superstar. I wished

I'd had fun every day, instead of being so obsessed with who would give me a medal at the end of it.

I wished I'd figured it all out sooner.

But I still had one more night and the tournament to make it right.

I checked my watch and saw that there were only a couple of minutes left before my final basketball session started. I jogged the rest of the way back, ready to make some changes.

"Where were you?" Jackson asked when I met up with him on the court.

"Just doing some thinking."

"Coach wants us to split into teams for a scrimmage."

"Then let's pull some guys together," I said, scanning the group.

None of them would look at me.

I took a deep breath, knowing that was my own fault.

"Jackson?"

"Yeah?"

"Can you convince anyone to play with me?"

It was a pretty embarrassing thing to have to ask, but I'd put myself in that position.

"Definitely," he said, sounding way more sure of it than I was.

It took a few minutes (which felt like hours while I stood by myself and felt like a loser), but Jackson managed to talk Big Mike, Danny, and T. J. into joining us.

"Hey," I said, to the group, but all I got back was one nod from Danny.

At least it was a start.

We got into position and even though I wanted to be a forward, I let the other guys have the prime positions and moved to guard.

Be less aggressive.

When Coach blew his whistle, the other guys won the tip-off and started dribbling down the court toward me.

I got into a crouch and kept my eyes on the ball.

When it got close enough, I made my move and with one lightning-fast strike, I had it.

I knew that if I'd had possession just a day earlier, I would have gone for the basket.

Don't be a ball hog.

I looked left, then right, getting a feel for where my teammates were. I thought back to Pioneer practice with Coach Baxter and how he'd wanted us to make five passes before a shot.

That felt like ten million years ago.

I couldn't see past the waving arms, so I called out, "Who's open?"

There was stunned silence for a few seconds, then I heard Big Mike shout, "Over here!"

I passed him the ball and jogged down the court, concentrating not only on it, but on where my teammates were.

Big Mike took a shot that bounced off the rim, but T. J. caught the rebound.

"I'm open!" I shouted.

He hesitated, then threw me the ball. I bounced it a couple of times. All I wanted to do was find a clear *shot*, but I ignored the basket and found a clear *pass* instead.

I tossed the ball to Danny, who looked totally shocked for a second, then nodded once and went for the hoop.

The ball bounced off the backboard and dropped right through the net.

"Nice one!" I called out to him, clapping a couple of times as I ran back down the court.

The next time we had the ball, I let Jackson take the shot, then Danny. I passed every time I had the chance and didn't go for the points once.

"What's going on?" Big Mike asked when we took a five-minute break.

"We're winning," I told him, with a shrug.

"No, what's going on with *you*?"

I cleared my throat. "I'm trying to be a better teammate."

"Cool," he said. "You know, you're a pretty awesome player when you're not showboating."

I guess I knew who'd made *that* comment.

The word still stung a bit, but I knew it was true.

"Thanks."

"Yeah," Danny said. "You keep this up and we're golden tomorrow."

"Don't worry," I told them. "I'll keep it up."

"Awesome," Danny said, giving me a high five.

And it was.

On Friday morning, I woke up feeling kind of bummed that it was the last day of camp. Then I lay in bed for a few minutes, thinking about the awesome prank we'd pulled the night before.

Plastic wrap on the doors. I swear, my brother was a genius.

I showered and got dressed, then stopped by Jackson's room so we could hit the cafeteria together.

"Are you okay?" I asked when I saw his face.

He had huge bags under his eyes, like he hadn't slept at all.

"Yeah. I'm just nervous about playing in front of my dad."

"Really?" I couldn't imagine feeling that way about my own dad.

"He'll tell me I did a great job, like he always does. But this time I want it to be true."

"Hey, you played awesome yesterday."

"You think so?" he asked, like he didn't believe me.

"Definitely. The five of us make a good team."

He was quiet for a minute. "You know, he'll be pretty

happy that I made some friends this time. Like, real friends, you know?"

I nodded, knowing exactly what he meant.

After a short session in the morning, all of the campers had to go back to the dorm to pack up their stuff so we'd be ready to leave after the tournament.

I had to get three guys to sit on my suitcase, just so I could zip it up. I hadn't even worn half the stuff I brought!

Around ten o'clock, the parents started to show up.

After Mom and Dad gave me and Russ some huge hugs (I would have been embarrassed, but all of the other parents were doing the exact same thing), Dad headed over to the gym with me while Mom and Russ left for his Olympic thing.

"Did you have a good time?" Dad asked, while we were crossing the courtyard.

"Definitely," I told him. "I learned a lot."

How weird that I wasn't talking about basketball.

I helped Dad find a spot in the bleachers and was about to head down to the court, when he said, "Whoa! Is that Roberto Farina?"

"Yeah," I said, taking a peek at Jackson's dad. The guy was huge! "His son was here for camp."

When I met up with my teammates down on the floor,

we only had a couple of minutes until the tip-off for the first game.

"Are we ready to do this?" I asked the guys.

"Totally," Danny said, while the others nodded.

I noticed that Jackson still looked totally freaked out.

We made it through the first game like it was nothing. Our communication was awesome, the ball handling was sweet, and the points just kept coming.

I concentrated really hard on passing the ball to whoever had the best shot.

"You need to shoot, too, Owen," T. J. said when we took a break.

"Yeah," Danny said. "You've gotta go for it."

I listened to what they said and when we got back to the game, I took the shots I was sure of, but passed when I wasn't.

Game two was a snap as well, and when it came down to the final showdown between us and the remaining team, I felt like the tournament was ours.

We played like a well-oiled machine, and it didn't even matter whether I was the piece that scored or assisted.

It just felt awesome to be part of it.

But when it came down to the final seconds, we were tied.

T. J. dribbled down the court and passed to Big Mike, who spun around to lose a guard. He passed to Danny and I matched their pace. Once we got close to the basket, I realized that I was wide open.

I didn't have to say anything, because Danny saw me and hurled the ball.

The game-winning shot would be the easiest one of the day.

I couldn't believe it was mine to take!

And that's when I saw Jackson.

Obviously, I'm all about winning. I'm into scoring baskets and making plays. But in that second, I realized that every now and then you have to take a time-out.

"Jackson!" I shouted, holding up the ball.

He blinked hard and stared at me until he realized what I was doing. Surprised, he lifted his hands in the air.

I sent the ball flying over a sea of arms and straight to my target.

And in the final two seconds on the clock, he took the shot.

Swish.

He won the game for us.

We all started jumping around and whooping, but as loud as we were, I swear I heard Roberto Farina cheering over the rest of the crowd.

I stood next to Jackson while the awards for the week

were handed out. And when Roberto Farina put the MVP medal around T. J.'s neck, I didn't even mind.

Well, of course I *minded*. I wanted it for myself. But the thing was, no one should get an award for *one day* of doing the right thing. An MVP got it right all the time—in practice, at game time, and even off the court.

T. J. was the right choice.

When it was all over, every camper was smiling, knowing what an awesome week it had been.

"Thank you, Owen," Jackson said as I started to head toward the stairs to meet Dad.

"You're the one who scored," I reminded him.

"You know what I mean."

And I did.

"Hey, can I get your phone number or e-mail or whatever?" I asked. "I want to stay in touch with the team."

"Sure."

We shared contact info with each other and the pranksters, all of us promising to try to come back next year.

"So," Jackson said once we were alone in the crowd. He looked over at his dad, who was surrounded by people shaking his hand and asking for autographs. The NBA star kept moving toward Jackson, wearing a gigantic smile. "I guess you want to meet my dad."

I thought about what it would be like to wonder if people only liked you because of who your dad was.

It would totally stink.

As much as I wanted to meet the legendary Roberto Farina, pose for a photo with him, and shake his hand, I let it go.

"Nah," I said.

Jackson blinked hard. "Seriously?"

"Yeah," I told him. "Maybe I can meet him at camp next year or something."

"For sure," he said, grinning.

I said good-bye and watched Jackson cut through the crowd. I smiled when Roberto Farina, NBA superstar, lifted his kid off the ground in a huge hug.

It was pretty cool.

"Hey," Dad said, from behind me.

I turned around and he gave me a high five, then a hug of my own.

When he let go, he said, "Mom just texted to say that Russ got the award for most improved athlete."

"Cool," I said, grinning. My brother, the *athlete*.

"So, are you ready to head out?"

"Yeah. No, wait! Do you have your camera?"

"I sure do," he said, pulling it out of his pocket.

"Can you take a picture of me?" I glanced at the crowded court, then back at Dad. "And maybe catch Farina in the background?"

Putting Jackson's feelings first didn't mean I had to walk away empty-handed.

When Dad got the perfect shot, we walked toward the stairs.

"You know, you were pretty amazing out there, O," he said, rubbing my head. "I'm really proud of you."

"It's just basketball," I told him.

"Hey," he said, looking me in the eye. "That last pass was a lot bigger than basketball."

I turned to see Jackson grinning at his father and knew Dad was right.

Some things really were bigger than basketball.

Not a *lot* of things, but *some*.

Acknowledgments

I'd like to thank my Kiwi agent, Sally Harding, for our twelve-year partnership and the eleven books she has guided to publication (so far!).

Huge thanks as well to the fine folks at the Cooke Agency for their kindness and diplomacy when dealing with fretful authors.

And finally, I'd like to give big shout-outs to Nicole Gastonguay, designer of three amazing covers for the Athlete vs. Mathlete series, and to Bloomsbury's copyediting team for making sense of it all.

W. C. Mack is the author of all the books in the Athlete vs. Mathlete series, including *Athlete vs. Mathlete* and *Double Dribble*, as well as numerous books for children. Raised in Vancouver, she now lives in Portland, Oregon.

www.wcmack.com